"Marilee Hart," I said. "I just don't believe this."

"This isn't any accident, is it?" she said. She had worry, not welcome, written all over her face.

"Huh?"

"Robin, what's going on? Are they looking for me? Are you alone?"

"You mean now?" I asked. "Or in Mexico? I'm alone right now, but Jeet is here with me in Mexico. See, I'm going around to horse farms and . . ."

"Looking for me," she said.

I was totally disconcerted. "Well, no."

"What are you doing here then?" she asked.

It was only then that I noticed what she had in her hands. It was a sawed-off shotgun.

I gestured at it and laughed. "Well," I said, "at least you aren't going to need that."

She didn't laugh back. "For your sake," she said, "I hope you're right. . . ."

By Carolyn Banks:

THE TURTLE'S VOICE
TART TALES: Elegant Erotic Stories
PATCHWORK
THE GIRLS ON THE ROW
THE DARKROOM
MR. RIGHT
THE ADVENTURES OF RUNCIBLE SPOON
THE HORSE LOVER'S GUIDE TO TEXAS
     (coauthor)
A LOVING VOICE: A Caregiver's Book of Read-
     Aloud Stories for the Elderly (coeditor)
A LOVING VOICE II: A Caregiver's Book of More
     Read-Aloud Stories for the Elderly (coeditor)
DEATH BY DRESSAGE*
GROOMED FOR DEATH*
MURDER WELL-BRED*

Published by Fawcett Books

MURDER
WELL-BRED

Carolyn Banks

FAWCETT GOLD MEDAL • NEW YORK

A Fawcett Gold Medal Book
Published by Ballantine Books
Copyright © 1995 by Carolyn Banks

All rights reserved under International and Pan-American Copyright Conventions. Published in the United States by Ballantine Books, a division of Random House, Inc., New York, and simultaneously in Canada by Random House of Canada Limited, Toronto.

Library of Congress Catalog Card Number: 95-90432

ISBN 0-449-14914-5

Manufactured in the United States of America

First Edition: December 1995

10 9 8 7 6 5 4 3 2 1

Author's Note

I want to thank William Browning Spencer, Janis Rizzo, Jeff Hartman, Diane Payton Gomez, Paula Tremblay, and Karen Langston for their critical reading of this manuscript.

I'd also like to thank the people of San Miguel de Allende, Mexico, especially Nonie Mulcaster and Robert and Ma Eugenia Moir.

And as always, I'm grateful to my editor, Elisa Wares, and my agent, Vicky Bijur.

Carolyn Banks

For Jeff Hartman,
a tough critic and
a good friend.

CHAPTER 1

"Robin, are you absolutely sure?"

This was my husband, asking if I wanted him to come along with me while I schlepped around Guanajuato from one horse farm to another.

If you know Jeet at all, you know what a wrench it must have been for him to ask me that. Because if there's one thing Jeet can live without, it's horse farms. Horse farms and the horses that inhabit them.

"I'm sure," I said, my heart swelling the way your heart will swell when you have a sudden extra-big rush of love for someone.

But then he had to go and spoil it by wagging his finger at me. "Just remember," he warned, "you aren't in America. You have to be careful down here. It isn't—"

"Please, Jeet," I said. "You told me about the Napoleonic code about thirty-three times already. And I get it. Now relax. I'll be fine." I turned away and rolled my eyes. Honestly. You'd think I was fourteen years old!

"I'm not trying to be a pill," he said. "Mexican

1

prisons are the pits. You could get into one and never get out or—"

"I'm just driving to some horse farms," I interrupted. "It isn't as though I'm going to get involved in some international incident." Jeez.

"Driving is how it happens. You get in an accident and the next thing you know, you're in jail." He moved to the window of our hotel room and looked out into the street. "And I don't know if driving is a great idea," he said. "The streets are pretty darn narrow."

I knew he'd relent on this one: we'd paid a fortune to rent the car. No kidding. It cost more to rent the car than it did to fly here.

We were in San Miguel de Allende. It's this town in the mountains with no stoplights, no parking meters, no neon, no billboards, and ancient cobblestone streets. And all of it on purpose, too. It's a colonial city that the Mexican government wants to keep that way. Quaint, but really quaint, as opposed to fake. Tourists from all over—the U.S., Canada, Europe, even Asia—come here in droves.

I wanted to come the minute Jeet announced that his newspaper—the *Austin Daily Progress*—was sending him here. Jeet's the food critic. And because a lot of Texans travel to San Miguel, the paper wanted to do a piece on the local cuisine.

They weren't paying for me, of course. But Jeet got me sort of a gig so that I could come along tax-deductibly. What I was doing, sort of, was writing a story, just like Jeet. Except that while his was about food, mine was going to be about horses.

Horses are my thing.

When Jeet first suggested that I do this—that is, get an assignment to write a story about horse farms in central Mexico so that I could come along—I scoffed. Who would ever hire me? I'd taken honors English in college (in fact, that's where I'd first met Jeet) but—don't laugh—my major had been phys. ed.

But back to how I got this assignment.

Jeet had picked up a pile of horse magazines and waved them about. I subscribed to probably five or six. He opened one of them to the page where the people who work there are listed—the masthead, he called it—pointing to the editor's name. "Here," he said. "Call this person and say, 'I'm going to be in San Miguel de Allende, and I wondered if you'd like a story about . . .' "

"About what?" I'd asked.

"About whatever you think would be good. Horse farms or famous riders who live in the area. What would *you* want to read about?"

"There have been some famous teachers in San Miguel," I'd said. "Margaret Gaines, I think. She used to teach Pony Clubbers up in Canada and even made an Olympic rider or two. And Kathy Guertin, who was long-listed for the team a bunch of times. And right now there's some guy who wrote a famous equitation book."

So I'd called around and asked some people who'd been to San Miguel and eventually I got the name of the guy who wrote the book. Hans Bell.

I also got a list of farms. You know, places where there are shows or where people can board their horses or take lessons or whatever. Manuel—an old

man who works for Suzie Ballinger—told me about
a farm called Milagro (that's "miracle" to you grin-
gos). He'd never been there, but he'd heard about it
from bunches of people who'd come up from Mexico,
he'd said.

So, armed with all this information, I did what
Jeet suggested, called the editor of *Horse Play*, and
guess what? I was now Robin Vaughan, freelance
journalist, Brenda Starr and Lois Lane and Oriana
Fallaci all rolled into one. I still get the giggles
whenever I think about it: me, actually working.

Oh, please, don't write me nasty letters. I know
women work. It's just that I never have, unless you
count the couple of weeks I tried to hustle makeup
door-to-door. There just isn't anything out there for
a slightly overweight phys. ed. major, you know
what I mean? Plus our little Primrose Farm would
absolutely fall apart if it weren't for me and my
trusty hammer, wrench, and posthole digger.

Okay, okay, you're right. I'm getting defensive.
But the point is that I'm here in Mexico legiti-
mately. On business. Just like Jeet. I'm here in
Mexico to do a *Horse Play* story about horse farms.
The car had been rented at our own expense just
for me. Jeet would be able to hoof it to the places
he had to see. Restaurants like Mama Mia and El
Harem—not very native, to be sure. But that's the
way San Miguel is, offering everything from Italian
to Lebanese cuisine.

"Keep track of your expenses," Jeet was saying.

I had more or less tuned him and his list of cau-
tions out and had just now tuned back in. "I will,"
I promised, looking into my Sportsac to make sure

I had my pen and my notebook and my Spanish phrase book and my tape recorder and my map of Guanajuato.

Guanajuato is the state that San Miguel de Allende is in.

"And make sure that you take enough pesos." Digging in his pockets now and doling out some paper money and some coins as well. There were old pesos and nuevo pesos, so that it was doubly confusing. I just planned not to spend anything, although the place is filled with stores that tempt you with gorgeous handwoven shawls and dresses and things.

But I loved going in and out of the stores. The shopkeepers sit in the dark until you walk in, and then the lights go on, which in a way makes you feel really special.

I guess I had a flash of insecurity on my way out the door and it showed, because Jeet laughed and walked over to ruffle my bangs. "You'll do just fine as a reporter," he said. Or maybe, come to think of it, he was reassuring himself, not me at all.

Minutes later I was climbing into the Ford Fiesta we had rented and easing out into what passed for traffic in this burg. Which meant I pretty much had the road to myself.

I wondered why everyone in the U.S. talked about auto accidents all of the time. Because the cars that went clattering past me were absolute wrecks. We're talking *Road Warrior* here, I mean rusted-out seventies American cars that somehow had eluded the compacter. I mean, if you ran into one of those, who would be able to tell?

Unless our hotel was just in a crummy part of town.

I had suspected this and worse of our hotel. For one thing, it advertised that it had hot water twenty-four hours a day. This, I thought, is a high point? Still, it was what Jeet's newspaper was paying for. Well, all right. So some Austin paper can't be expected to rival *The New York Times* in perks. Still, *hot water*?

But even if the hotel was in a lesser neighborhood, it was beautiful. I'm talking flowers upon flowers, heaps of bougainvillea and lantana and trumpet vine spilling out over high stucco walls. That and lots of tile. Tile that you'd pay maybe five bucks a tiny little square for back home, used on everything: walls and benches and planters and floors.

The streets are a maze, and there's an odd kind of equality, with the houses bunched right up against each other, and what goes on in them hidden behind high walls and huge old battered wooden doors. Sometimes a door will open and you'll catch a glimpse of either squalor or splendor, the two often side by side. And it's totally unpredictable which it will be from the outside.

There are *fuentes*—which are fountains—all over the place. And birds. Bright-colored birds that perched on things as if the chamber of commerce had hired them to do it.

Beautiful.

I wasn't alone in being charmed by the place. A

lot of Americans are. A lot of English-speaking people live here permanently. I forget the actual number, but a lot. Enough to have their own phone book (called, I kid you not, the *Juarde*, as in, "Who are they?").

Oh, I know, you're thinking cheaper. But it isn't. I don't know anything about economics, but a man on the plane—an American who had retired here—said you'd need about forty thou bare minimum just to make ends meet. So cheap it ain't.

I guess it's the gorgeousness that gets them, then. That and the climate, which is said to be kind of like the temperatures you get in San Francisco, never too hot, never too cold, go sleeveless in the daytime and get your Fair Isle sweaters out at night.

God. I was sounding like a tour guide.

But the thing is, I'm not exactly a world traveler. At the risk of sounding like an old Three Dog Night song, I've never been much of anywhere. Never been to England or France. Never been to Germany or Greece. Actually, it would be a lot easier to tell you where I *have* been.

To Spain, once, with my parents when I was thirteen. To Spain and that's it, unless you count Canada, though only to whatever is on the other side of Niagara Falls. I think I was thirteen then, too.

Thirteen must have been the year my wanderlust kicked in and shipped back out.

Because I'm in my thirties now, and except for a trip to New York City that I made with Jeet last year, that's it.

I'm not complaining. I mean, I like my life, like

my routine. I like our little four-acre Primrose
Farm, like my horses, Plum and Spier. I like Austin, the low-key blue-jeans-and-sneakers attitude
that exists there.

But still, you can see why I leaped at the chance
to come to a place I'd heard about for years, a kind
of mountain paradise, a sanctuary for writers and
painters. Even Clifford Irving lived here, I think.

By now I'd reached a part of town that seemed,
well, not a part of *town*. Instead of being all
scrunched together (albeit in a picturesque kind of
way), the houses had space around them, little
lawns, more like suburban homes. I kept driving
and now came by a few even farther apart that
were nicely fenced with board or smooth wire.

I knew what that meant: horse country.

My heartbeat increased.

Dumb, yes, but what can I say? That's the way it
is for me. I can be in the worst mood imaginable
and feel instantly cheered by the sight of a horse.
I'm not alone in this feeling. Horses would never
have survived if they didn't have this effect on huge
numbers of folks. Even brushing a horse can re-
store your spirits, and having one flap its velvet
lips over the palm of your hand, well, that's a piece
of heaven.

In this case, however, I was also cheered by the
sight of the farm I was about to visit, all white
stucco with a red tile roof and huge, ancient timber
beams. This was Hans Bell's place, Reitenhof, and
the sign in front announced that fact.

Reitenhof. Old Hans hadn't exactly acclimated to
his surroundings, you might say.

Of course, that was one of the things that had amused me as I'd wandered around town with Jeet. You'd see little tiled signs on the houses naming the owners, and the owners were anything but Mexican.

Casa Bernstein ... Casa Guttmacher ... Casa O'Brien ...

You don't think that's funny?

Well how about Casa Dr. Scholl's?

Because there is one and I was very glad to see it after we'd hiked up what has to be a hill as steep as any in the Andes.

But I digress.

Here I was at that little old hacienda, Reitenhof, staring at a pair of huge wooden doors, I mean twice the size of regular doors, with big black wrought-iron door knockers on them.

All I could think of was *Young Frankenstein*, when my mother took me to see it. The guy says, "What knockers!" and this actress—was it Teri Garr?—blushes and looks down at her cleavage and says, "Oh, thank you, doctor." I don't know how old I was, but young enough not to want my mother to know that I'd gotten the joke.

Still, I had to be careful not to comment on the knockers if a woman answered the door.

But a woman didn't. A boy did. He was about fourteen, with huge brown eyes and the whitest teeth I'd ever seen. "Dr. Bell is expecting," he said.

I thought of Arnold Schwarzenneger right away, but I resisted comment and followed him through a warren of high-ceilinged rooms, rooms with a museumlike feel to them, what with the statuary and the massive furniture and all.

No kidding. I felt absolutely tiny here. At one point I asked the boy to stop so I could look at a massive carved chair. It had been made, the boy said, from mesquite. To Texans, mesquite is a plague, a thorny never-say-die tree that will sprout wherever you don't want it—your pasture, your arena. I think we started burning it in our grilles to kind of get even with it. But here was furniture, beautiful furniture, made from the stuff. And you know I'm not into home furnishings, don't you? So you know this had to be really special.

But not so special that I'd want to live in this house. It was stiff and way too formal, right down to the huge ancestral (I surmised) portraits on the walls. Military men, mostly, and all wearing disapproving looks.

Even though the house wasn't dark, it felt dark. There were thick tapestry drapes pulled closed, and carpeting that absorbed even tiny sounds. It just didn't seem Mexican, by which I mean airy, bright, fanciful.

But then we came to the courtyard and I had to take it all back. Herr Bell's decorative hand had not been applied out here. It was elaborately tiled, with a three-tiered percolating fountain and maybe twenty trees bearing actual oranges and limes. There were bright-plumed parrots in cages, who regarded us as we walked by. I'll tell you, if a mariachi band had been playing, I wouldn't have been at all surprised.

We went through the length of it, down a wide

flight of stairs, through a series of ornate gates, and into the stable area.

White stucco, dark wood with wrought-iron trim, red tiled roof. Flowering vines growing up the side. I mean, heaps and heaps of flowers, orange and yellow and fuchsia. Hummingbirds darting around, fighting each other for position at the blossoms.

This is more like it, I thought. Followed by, I wish Jeet had come. I knew that I could describe this place to him all day long and still never do it justice.

Unless this was typical down here.

"You will wait, I get Herr Bell," the boy said, thrusting me into what was obviously the trophy room, before disappearing.

So there I was, surrounded by glass shelves bearing silver cups and statuettes and medallions and ribbons. There were also photographs—the same man, elegant and aristocratic, on dozens of equally aristocratic horses.

The man had done it all. There were show jumping pictures, cross-country pictures, foxhunting pictures, dressage pictures. Underneath each photo was an elaborately scripted pedigree—the family tree of whatever horse was pictured taken back through several generations.

But to return to the man, who I could only assume was Hans Bell. His seat was impeccable, his hands and legs, too. The horses beneath him looked correct—maybe rigidly so.

But hey. Who am I to judge? This guy had obviously been involved with every aspect of the horse biz all of his life, and successfully, too.

There were several pictures of him on those steplike things they use in the Olympics to award medals. There he was, at various ages, medallions being placed around his neck.

Then the door to the room flew open and I was faced with the man himself.

Hans Bell. The kind of man you quite literally have to look up to. I mean, super tall.

I glanced back at the photographs, wondering how huge the horses in them must have been. Think Budweiser here, though the horses weren't as thick-bodied as the Budweiser Clydesdales. No. They were light, refined by comparison. But—I glanced back at the photos—so wooden!

"I'm Robin Vaughan," I said, fighting the urge to stammer.

"Of course," he said, which I thought was very odd.

He was very handsome, with angular features and fashionably slicked-back hair. He was actually wearing jodhpurs, you know those baggy breeches that you see in old cavalry films, the kind that mushroom out over the top of your riding boots, like the ones Faye Dunaway wore in *Chinatown*. He looked as terrific as she did in them.

I held my hand up and he—I swear—clicked his heels together and sort of dipped down into a bow over it. Something clanked as he did so.

I glanced down at his feet and saw the rowels of his spurs cross.

"I have your book," I said, wishing I'd forced myself to slog through it. I had really tried, but the prose was impenetrable. I was willing to blame the translation.

, "Yes." But he hadn't put a question mark at the end of it, as if eager for my assessment.

"Uh . . ." I tried. What now? I mean, I'd been with Jeet when he interviewed people, and he never seemed to come up against a wall like this. I mean, it was probably an imaginary wall, but still. What was it, interviewer's block? "So, uh, are you, like, writing right now?" I fished through my bag as I spoke and finally found my tape recorder.

"No," he said, his eyes narrowing with impatience. "Right now I am overseeing the incompetent local horse-shoer. Come along."

I followed him through the arched doorway where the boy had gone and came out where the horses—six of them—were cross-tied to pillars.

"Do you just have the one book?" I asked.

"This interview is about my horses, is it not?" he asked.

"Well, uh, yes," but I'd wanted to break the ice a little. Kind of establish that I knew something about him. I mean, I'd seen Jeet do that. "Your book was about riding," I said, kind of stubbornly.

"I have had the horses readied for you," he said. "I assume you will want to photograph them."

"Oh."

He waited, I guess for me to produce a camera.

"I don't take photographs," I said. "I write. I mean, I'm writing this story and everything. Not that I'm actually a writer." I laughed haltingly. "I mean, my husband is actually the writer."

"And is your husband with you?"

"In Mexico, yes. But not here, not now. I mean, he writes about food and I'm supposed to be, you know, writing about horses."

I don't know. I do dither around a lot, especially when I feel uncomfortable, but now I felt completely inept. Like some student reporter or something.

And I could tell by the way he was staring at me that he wasn't about to be charmed by it.

But then he came to some kind of decision. As though he would proceed with the task no matter how unpleasant. Kind of like telling the dentist, "Okay, you can drill on me now."

"Well, then," he said, making a sweep with his hand to indicate the six horses that stood cross-tied before us.

I felt as though I ought to genuflect.

They were beautiful animals, tall and muscled as though they were worked nearly every day. They had been groomed to perfection, coats shining, manes trimmed short, tails without a tangle or snarl. Their hooves were bright with hoof dressing and they stood obediently and square. Not a one had a leg carelessly cocked the way horses at rest often do.

Because they weren't at rest, I realized. Not with Herr Bell in the vicinity.

I could see the wary eyes in the horse that was closest to me, an enormous bay. I watched the way she followed his every movement. When she was being ridden, her body would probably do the same. She'd be ready to follow any change, even the most subtle, in her rider's posture, maybe even her rider's breathing.

Caballo preparado. The ready horse. That was how Herr Bell had referred to it in his text. Unfortunately, though, the readiness I was witnessing seemed borne of fear. Still, I was about to make a reference to that phrase of his when he spoke.

"You have horses?" he asked me.

I nodded. I thought I'd mention Plum first, then knock his socks off by telling him about Spier. "I have a Thoroughbred off the track—" I'd managed to begin before he cut me off.

"This is what I think of Thoroughbreds," Herr Bell said, and spit.

I was stunned. I had a childish urge to say, Oh, yeah? Well, this is what I think of *your* horses, and start spitting back. Except that I knew that would be a really dumb thing to do. And besides. His horses really were above such comment.

And spitting is a guy thing anyway. I don't think I've ever seen a woman spit. On the other hand, I once saw a high-ranking U.S. Army officer spit while walking down a public street.

Come to think of it, Jeet doesn't spit. And none of Jeet's male cronies do either. So maybe it's not just a guy thing, but an older-guy thing.

At any rate, Herr Bell took the practice to a new level. Because after he spit, he snapped his fingers and pointed to the tiles where his sputum had landed. And then Miguelito, the boy who'd opened the door, knelt and mopped at the spot with a cloth.

Oy, I thought, but forced myself to smile at Herr Bell anyway.

He did not smile back. It was then that I noticed the deep frown lines that were etched into his face. I didn't think it had much to do with the hot Mexican sun.

And he wouldn't let go of what I'd said. "I would not have a Thoroughbred," he continued. "An American Thoroughbred especially. Bah!"

He wasn't kidding, either.

"Different strokes," I offered. I still had what I hoped was a reasonably pleasant expression frozen on my face, but I feared that it looked blatantly artificial. Did you ever see the horror movie *Dr. Sardonicus*? It was kind of like that.

Or like Gloria Vanderbilt going, "Here, these are my teeth." Anyway.

Bell's eyes scrunched up, as if he were trying to decipher my statement before challenging or dismissing it. It's true, it must've sounded puzzling to a foreigner.

". . . for different folks," I added, far too late. I didn't think he was up for a lengthy conversation about the old songs of Sly and the Family Stone.

"These animals," he said, gesturing back at his own horses again, "are *bred* for the sport of dressage."

He pointed, as if I were oblivious to the horses' various brands. "Holsteiner," he said, going down the line, "Holsteiner, Hanoverian, Hanoverian, Westphalian, Oldenburg."

I nodded as I followed him along the walkway. I mean, I wasn't going to argue. Lord knows I'd had my problems with Plum, maybe problems that stemmed from the fiery nature of the Thoroughbred breed. I dunno. All I do know is, I don't like blanket dismissals of any kind, and especially blanket dismissals of horses I own.

"Breeding is everything," Herr Bell allowed, his eyes boring in on me.

I stood there, that dopey grin still fixed on my face.

Then I cheered myself up by comparing the way my horses acted when they saw me to the way Herr Bell's horses were at the sight of him.

Night and day.

My horses make soft nickering noises.

His were mute.

But beyond that, they all changed very subtly when Herr Bell walked past. They went from looking neutral to looking nasty. Not killer nasty, just, I don't know, ears sort of back, which never means anything good.

It was a definite mood swing.

You could also tell that if they knew what was good for them, they'd better not act on their evil intentions. I know, it sounds like a snap judgment on my part, but believe me, it isn't. I've been around horses forever, and I can pretty much tell what they're thinking.

I'm not pretending clairvoyance. It's just that horses are pretty transparent. To my mind, that's one of the nicest things about them.

I found myself thinking about something that happened to me at a clinic once, and wished Herr Bell had been the kind of person I could have shared it with.

What happened was that Plum took a great dislike to one woman's horse. Every time the horse came near Plum, she would pin her ears back. She'd have happily kicked the other horse to kingdom come if I hadn't been on her, reminding her not to with my legs.

The woman told me I should wallop Plum with my crop.

"Why?" I asked. "She hasn't done anything bad."

"But she *wants* to," the woman said.

The woman gave up on me and actually complained to the clinician—a Canadian named Stewart—about Plum's attitude.

Stewart walked up to me. In fairness, he'd noted, as had everyone else in the clinic, what a jerk this woman was. So right in front of her, he asked, "Has Plum kicked out?"

"No," I told him.

"And is Plum a Catholic horse?"

"A *Catholic* horse?" I thought he was losing it.

"Roman Catholic," he explained.

"No," I said, hearing the old *Twilight Zone* theme somewhere off in the distance.

But then Stewart turned to the woman. "Plum is not a Catholic horse," he told her. "She therefore cannot be punished for the intention." And then he flashed a smug smile at me—the memory of which I'll treasure until I die.

Of course there was no point relaying any of this to Bell. And so I didn't.

Especially since I could tell he was mad that I wasn't able to take pictures.

We ended up beside a leather-aproned blacksmith who had the rear foot of the last horse in line resting on a small metal stand. He was filing away the hoof that overhung the shoe.

Bell said nothing to him, but to me he said, "My regular man is away. *This* is what I'm forced to use."

The shoer continued filing, while I squirmed.

I consoled myself by thinking that probably the shoer didn't speak any English, but there was no mistaking Hans Bell's tone. The poor man would have to be deaf.

But Bell didn't want him not to get it. He got close to the man and said, "You have ignored what I told you about the angle of the hoof."

The shoer didn't alter the expression on his face. He kept filing.

Bell went even closer, putting his face practically into the smithy's and lowering his voice in a way that gave me shivers. "You will acknowledge my remark," he said.

The mare swayed back away from him. She was too well trained to yank her foot away from the shoer, but she clearly didn't like Hans Bell's ominous tone.

I didn't like it either. I thought, too, he was probably tempering things with me there. He'd have flogged the guy, probably, if I hadn't been along.

The blacksmith finished filing, put the hoof down, and straightened. He turned. He was a foot shorter than Herr Bell, at least. He stared up at the man, his face unreadable.

The mare watched warily, as did I.

"Miguelito," Herr Bell said, snapping his fingers. The houseboy, who'd been standing in the shadows all this time, came forward and began rooting through in the blacksmith's wooden toolbox.

The boy found a measuring device and applied it, fingers fumbling, to the mare's hoof.

I wondered what would happen if the blacksmith were off by even half a degree.

"Is perfect," Miguelito announced, looking fearful.

Bell snatched the device with one hand, pushing Miguelito aside with the other. Then he bent and applied it himself. "So," he said, when he learned that the angle was right.

The blacksmith's expression went from blank to triumphant.

Herr Bell did the heel-click thing again. The rowels of his spurs touched. "So," he said again, backing two steps away.

Not, "I'm sorry," you'll notice, but "So." I imagined him getting his spurs tangled up and falling flat on his face. I'd have willed it if I could.

The mare, who had been tense the whole while Hans Bell was standing near, visibly relaxed as he moved away.

Remind me never to ride with this guy, I thought. I reached forward and stroked the mare's gleaming shoulder and she leaned into it, grateful for my touch.

"So," I said, glad to have thought of a question at last. "You were a medallist at how many Olympics?"

"All of that information is available. You do not need to speak to me in order to gather it," he said.

"Yeah, well, a good journalist always confirms everything," I said, thinking, What a great save!

"I have been a patient man," Herr Bell said. "But my riding record has been published many times. I do not care to repeat that information. Now then, I would like you to ask me a question worthy of an answer."

Was it my imagination or did everything tense up again? I mean everything, Herr Bell, the blacksmith, the houseboy, the mare.

"Have you heard of a farm called Milagro?" I asked, glad to have something occur to me. It seemed pertinent, especially since he'd made that breeding-is-everything comment.

He looked at me with an expression that verged on contempt. "No," he said.

"Oh, well." I shrugged. "Let's see. . . ."

"I think I have given you time enough," he told me.

"But I just—"

"Miguelito will show you out."

"But . . ."

But nothing. Herr Bell wanted his reporters a lot more on the ball than I had been. And heck. I couldn't really blame him. I mean, as an asker of questions, I had been pretty bad. And I don't understand it. I mean, in normal conversation, I think I can ask more than my rightful share. On the other hand, no sense being too hard on myself. I mean, it was my first time out of the chute. Next time I'd write some questions down so that if my mind went blank it wouldn't matter. Still, I felt awfully embarrassed.

"Señora?" It was Miguelito, looking up at me.

Well, he'd be sympathetic, wouldn't he?

I searched his eyes. Was he contemptuous of me now, too?

I smiled. "Herr Bell's one tough cookie," I said.

He did not smile back. Instead, he increased his speed so that he could get me to the door and out of there all the faster.

I left Reitenhof in ignominy.

I sat in the car and stewed. I had the whole fiasco on tape, so I could play it for Jeet and maybe get some pointers. Except that right then I remembered something Jeet had told me that I hadn't heeded. A basic something at that. It was: Never ask a question that the person can answer yes or no to.

So I wouldn't play the tape for Jeet, because he'd only start lecturing me about how I hadn't been listening when he'd given me tips.

In fact, I might as well erase the tape, or rewind it, at least, so that I could tape right over it. No sense wasting good acetate.

On the other hand, maybe it didn't sound so bad. Maybe I could play it for my husband after all.

I flipped the play button and listened, wincing at what I heard. It was an abysmal interview, textbook bad. I rewound again and started back to town.

I tried to get into the scenery and forget how miserably I'd failed.

And the scenery was cool, all right. There were

major rocks. And there were odd cactus trees—yes, trees—shaped like umbrellas that had been turned upside down. There was eucalyptus, too, and day-blooming jasmine.

And there were the darnedest fences here in what I had to assume was the low-rent district. I saw one made entirely out of mattress springs, maybe a hundred of them rusting all in a row. A tumbledown stone wall had thorny branches topping it, wads of them, nature's answer to barbed wire.

The houses here were few and far between, made of concrete block, mostly, with scraps of tin weighted down with tires and rocks and things.

Roosters and pigs roamed at will.

But wait a minute! I hadn't seen this stuff on my way *to* Reitenhof. So I'd obviously turned the wrong way. I was heading farther out of town, not toward San Miguel at all.

Well, easily remedied, I thought, glancing into my rearview mirror and seeing what had to be the sorriest little red pickup truck ever reflected in it. I slowed, expecting it to pass.

But the poor truck couldn't get up enough speed.

Well, I couldn't wait all day. I pulled off onto the highway, planning to make a U-turn after the truck rolled by.

Except that it didn't. It pulled off, too.

I squinted at the mirror, wondering if the truck had just coincidentally died when I'd pulled off.

That didn't seem likely. Then I figured it out. It was probably a bandito. Stories about driving in Mexico are filled with banditos. Banditos who

robbed busses on the highway much the way des-
peradoes used to rob the stagecoach. Banditos
wearing ski masks and carrying AK-47s.

Suddenly my vulnerability seemed all too appar-
ent. I mean, here I was, on a lonely road in a country where I didn't even speak the language. Oh
God.

I hit the gas so hard that I peeled out, made a U,
and roared past the truck, foiling whatever it was
for the nonce. I caught a glimpse of the truck in
profile as I passed it and wondered how much of a
success this particular bandito could be. I mean,
that heap!

But that heap swung around and was now right
behind me, even though I had the Fiesta up to
sixty-five.

Seventy.

Oh, my. The truck must have been souped up or
something. I careened around bends and it careened right behind me. I mean, burros and cows
out grazing paused to watch our progress.

Meanwhile I silently prayed: Please, no wrecks,
the imagined sound of a Mexican jail door slamming an amen.

Why hadn't I told Jeet that yes, yes, I wanted
him to come?

I hit the San Miguel city limits—at least the
point where the cobblestones began again—with
my tires asqueal. The car bounced and I braked se-
verely, just in time to miss a high curb on the right.
There was an overlook on my left. The city—its
rooftops and minarets and the giant pink-tinged ca-

thedral that was La Parroquia—beckoned from below.

Tourists! There were tourists in the overlook! Three men in crisp khaki pants and polo shirts. I lurched across in front of an oncoming bus and slid to a stop.

The pickup did the same, positioning itself conveniently between the tourists and me.

I hit the horn and sat there, my eyes closed, the heel of my hand pressing the alarm unrelentingly. I felt someone try the door. I opened my eyes. And there was the blacksmith who had been shoeing the horses at Reitenhof.

I hurled myself out at him. "Thank God you're here," I said, looking for the driver of the truck. "I'm being followed. I . . ."

Where were the tourists? They'd been there just a moment ago. And where was the driver? Unless . . .

I looked at the blacksmith. "That's *your* truck," I accused.

He glanced back at the truck and then looked back at me. A grin began to shape itself, but ever so slowly. The way grins shape themselves on the faces of villains in, oh, say, James Bond movies.

"Ah," he said, "sí."

CHAPTER 2

And so we faced off against each other, the blacksmith and me. Except that he was being exceedingly cheerful for a person about to . . .

What? Mayhem me in some evil-bandito way?

I remembered how he'd stood up to Herr Bell and I thought, I don't stand a chance. Still, I clenched my fists, bound and determined to make things as hard for him as I could.

But he burst into a huge grin. "I know where is Milagro," he said, kind of proud of himself for knowing.

"You do?"

"Sí. I follow so I can tell you."

"Oh." I screwed my face into what I hoped was an apologetic expression.

"Señora, you are all right?"

"What?"

"You are ill, no?"

"Ill? No, I'm just, I don't know. Sorry I drove the way I did. I mean, I thought you were a bandito."

"Ah, sí."

And he was still as cheerful as ever. As if he didn't at all mind being mistaken for a criminal.

"I draw it for you," he said, pulling a pencil from the pocket of his overalls and gesturing back at his truck. *"Momento,"* he said.

"Wait!" I reached for my Guanajuato map and handed it to him.

"Ah, sí," he said with enthusiasm.

He walked over to a wall and spread the map out on the ground. We both bent over it. He pointed to a place up the Queretaro highway. *"Aquí,"* he said. "You will see a long road heading back into the golden hill. Follow it until you can drive no more. Then you walk. When you can walk no more, you will see it. Milagro."

"And they breed horses there?"

"Sí. Many fine horses."

"And Herr Bell does not know of this?" I was starting to pattern my words after his. I hoped he hadn't noticed. It just happens to me, and I don't know why. If he had noticed, he didn't appear offended by it.

Something flickered over the blacksmith's face. *"Quizás,"* he said.

Quizás. Quizás. I'd heard the word before, but I couldn't remember what it meant. "What's your name?" I asked him. *"Cómo se llama?"*

"Felipe," he said. ". . . y . . ." He pointed at me.

"Robin," I told him. "Robin Vaughan."

We shook hands. "Missus Robin," he said, "you drive muy fast, no?"

"Sometimes," I said, sort of abashed.

"You must take care," he said. "There is danger."

For a moment I thought he, like Jeet, was about to launch into a lecture on the Napoleonic code, but

this time I was spared. He gave a little salute and
moved back toward his truck.

Quizás. The word came back to me. It meant
"perhaps." Well, that was about as noncommittal a
remark as a person could make.

I stood there until he rattled away. I could hear
him rattling, in fact, all the way down the hill.
Then I folded the map and looked out over San
Miguel.

It was such a beautiful place. Out of time, really.
Below me, for instance, was a man with two burros, on his way to market, probably. And beyond
him was a woman carrying her laundry on her
head, perhaps on her way to the public gardens,
where women from the villages came to avail themselves of free water. I could see a little queue, too,
outside one of the houses. I could imagine why. I'd
passed one such just yesterday, where folks had
lined up to buy fresh tortillas one of the locals had
made and was weighing on a small scale. A real
cottage industry.

God, I loved this place. It had a fairy-tale atmo-
sphere, what with the minarets and parapets and
little campaniles and domes. Oh, I knew, because
I'd asked, that these housed little water pumps, but
still, it was beautiful.

And to top it off, I'd found the fabled Milagro!
And almost without even trying.

I looked at my watch. I hadn't been gone nearly
long enough to convince Jeet that my interview
with Hans Bell had been a success. Why not drive
out to Milagro right now? Then, when Jeet asked
how it went, I could maybe have something positive

to report instead of the shambles that had been my interview with Herr Bell.

I checked the map and decided it was doable. And I mentally reviewed what Felipe had said. It was then that his words, "the golden hill," seemed, well, not quite as specific as one might like.

Except that when I got there, there was no mistaking it, because it *was* a golden hill, a hill alive with deep yellow-and-orange wildflowers, shelves of them it seemed, like long streaming golden ribbons in the breeze.

I turned onto the sandy road that led back into it and, as Felipe had told me, drove until things looked as though they called for four-wheel drive.

Then I began walking.

I looked back at where I'd parked the little Fiesta. I was sure it couldn't be seen from the road. And I was wondering, Is this smart? because I was, in fact, trespassing.

Oh, I know. You're thinking: Since when has Robin Vaughan balked at a little trespassing, except that all of Jeet's warnings—and now the blacksmith's, too—were clanging in my head. I could get shot. Or worse, arrested.

But wait. They were both talking about driving, right. I was being an alarmist here. So I pressed on.

Then I thought, What if whoever owns this place has dogs? Rottweilers, a brace of them, who, with teeth bared, would come running out to greet me.

I imagined trying to outrun them. And failing. And there I'd lie, with the Rottweilers snacking on me until they had their fill and the buzzards moving in to pick my bones.

Imagination is not always a plus.

And—wouldn't you know?—intruding on my reverie came the actual sound of barking. Oh, it wasn't a deep, Rottweiler kind of bark. No. It was a yip-yappy sort of thing, a yip-yap I was more or less familiar with at that.

Chihuahuas. Chihuahuas looking like wingless bats, their little eyes bugging out and their little vampire teeth flashing in the sunlight. Chihuahuas, six of them, coming at me full throttle.

I don't know why people keep big attack dogs, because Chihuahuas are faster, meaner, and probably cost a heck of a lot less to feed. They seem to have a kind of inborne strategic skill, too, with some of them going for your shins while the others work on your heels. Believe me, I know whereof I speak. I used to know someone who had a bunch of them.

Marilee Hart.

But I couldn't take the time to reminisce about Marilee because they were upon me, the Chihuahuas, darting in and out, and enjoying it, too.

I growled back at them and stomped my feet, and while it kept them from actually biting me, it did not stop them from taking turns running in and out so that I couldn't much progress.

"Shoo! Shoo!" I started yelling, meanwhile inching my way back in the direction of the car. The growling noises that I'd tried hadn't done a thing. "Shoo."

To hell with Milagro. To hell with my newfound career.

Except that at the rate I was moving, it would take until dinnertime to make it to the Fiesta.

If Stephen King had met these Chihuahuas, *Cujo* would not have been a St. Bernard.

I don't usually think about kicking dogs, but I started preparing extensive fantasies about kicking these. In fact, I could imagine booting them, one little hairless body after another, over some invisible goalpost. Of course, if I'd done that in real life, I'd have been consumed with guilt, but still . . . Thinking about it, at the moment, was the only good thing in my life.

Suddenly a woman's voice rang out. *"Basta!"* she shouted.

The dogs stopped instantly. They hung their little bat heads and began whining. I squinted at the woman, who had the sun behind her and appeared as one shimmering silhouette. My guardian angel.

"Hey, thanks," I called out. *"Muchas gracias."*

And to my wonder, she said, "Robin Vaughan? Is that you?"

I recognized the voice.

I said, "Marilee?"

"Oh, my God, it *is* you," she responded. Then she looked around as though she feared we'd been observed.

"Marilee Hart," I said. "I just don't believe this."

She'd come close enough for me to make out the look on her face. It was pained.

"This isn't any accident, is it?" she said.

"Huh?"

"Robin, what's going on? Are they looking for me? Are you alone?"

"You mean now?" I asked. "Or in Mexico? I'm alone right now, but Jeet is here with me in Mexico. See, I'm going around to horse farms and—"

"Looking for me," she said.

I was totally disconcerted. "Well, no. I did look for you in the beginning," I conceded. "I mean, I tried. But then everybody said you'd just run off and . . . I don't know. I just gave up."

"What are you doing here then?" she asked.

It was only then that I noticed what she had in her hands. It was a sawed-off shotgun.

I gestured at it and laughed. "Well," I said, "at least you aren't going to need that."

She didn't laugh back. "For your sake," she said, holding it down now at her side, "I hope you're right."

CHAPTER 3

It had been at least three years since I'd seen Marilee Hart, who had disappeared under very mysterious circumstances. Actually, things had gotten pretty mysterious even before she disappeared.

I'll tell you all about it.

It started, I guess, at the Groundhog Classic, which traditionally is the first dressage show of the season in Austin.

That's when you get to see what everybody's going to be showing that year.

I was showing nothing, but Lola, who is my best friend, was showing four horses. Lo makes her living buying and selling horses, so she always has something new, a horse she's bringing along—often a rehab, a bad character who, under Lo's tutelage, has reformed.

Lo had enlisted me for the show as her groom, which meant that I got the horses ready for her to ride and led them off when she was done. I also watched her in the warm-up arena and shouted helpful things like, "He's not tracking up," and "You're leaning too far forward when you ask for the canter."

This sounds pretty stupid, but dressage is a nitpicking kind of sport. If I hadn't been willing to do this for free, Lo would have paid me to do it.

But I'm getting off the subject here.

Okay, it's the Groundhog Classic. Lo gets on horse number one and says, "While I'm riding this guy, you can longe the big bay on the far side."

In response I do a Stepin Fetchit imitation. "Yez, ma'am," I say, and Lola laughs as I head off toward the row of stalls on the other side of the big indoor arena where the judge is watching the riders doing their tests.

See, that's the way a dressage show works. Each level has four progressively harder tests that call for specific movements. Each movement is scored from one to ten. Then you get an overall score, a percentage based on the accumulated scores.

It sounds dumb, I know, but so does golf when you try to explain it. I mean, you hit this little ball until you get it in the hole and then you go where there's another hole. . . .

So anyway, I went to get the bay. Got the bay. Tacked him up—that is, put his saddle and bridle on—grabbed the longe line and the side reins and the long longe whip, and went outside.

So here I am, about to start him on the circle—which is what longeing is, you standing on the ground while the horse moves in a circle around you—when all hell breaks loose.

The next thing I know, Marilee Hart is all puffy and red-faced and she's screaming at me about how I should get my slimy hands off her horse, and the next thing I know, she is undoing the buckles of the girth and throwing Lola's saddle on the ground and then she is snatching the horse away from me and striding off with him.

"You . . ." I am shaking with anger and trying to decide what to call her, but I can't think of anything that wouldn't be too cutting, because Marilee is as poor as a church mouse and lives in a little caretaker's trailer on a big cattle ranch.

In fact, "trailer girl" is the way I heard someone refer to her once.

If you've been around horses much, you are familiar with women and girls like Marilee. Well, usually that's what they are, way-better-than-average female riders who don't come from the usual horsey background. They kind of scruff out a living of some kind, maybe giving an occasional riding lesson or something, just so they can be around horses. They are dirt-poor in a sport that's thought to belong—and it may—to the very rich.

And they're always sort of looked down upon. It isn't overt, but it's there, or maybe I'm just especially tuned in to it because I'm not in either camp, the really poor or the really rich, and as a result I am a sort of neutral observer—someone who gets to overhear both sides.

Anyway, very occasionally one of these poor girls will marry into something resembling financial stability, but more often than not, as my husband pointed out one time, they render themselves pretty much unmarriageable—even undatable, because they surround themselves with animals. These are women who bring their dogs with them when you ask them over to dinner. Or women who can't go anywhere, because they feed six times a day.

And all they ever talk about is horses. I mean, horse minutiae. They describe to you, in detail, their last ride's every footfall. And when they aren't talking about riding, they're talking about stable management, vigorously debating, oh, the relative merits of rolled oats versus crimped, say, or of various forms of bedding.

In other words, they get really boring, really odd.

Marilee's case had been on the mild side. She could still maintain a reasonable conversation, for example. But it was happening to her.

By which I mean, she owned six absolutely fierce Chihuahuas and a sweetheart of a Doberdane (you can deduce the combination here). Plus assorted cats. You'd see her driving down the road with this menagerie in the back of her pickup truck all the time, so you could never quite get it up to say, "Hey, want to see a movie?" because you knew she had reached the stage where she couldn't be apart from these animals.

I'm not kidding.

But anyway, the moment I'm talking about here, at the Groundhog Classic horse show, there had been a sort of rumor circulating that Marilee was dating someone.

But it's miles from my mind as I am on the showgrounds picking Lola's saddle off the ground. I am royally ticked about this, because a saddle costs a fortune and Marilee ought to know better. Plus Lola's saddles are all Passiers, too, so they are worth two fortunes.

Inside my head, I'm whining that it isn't as though I was going to steal Marilee's horse! It was an honest mistake I had made. I mean, he was a big bay, but obviously not *the* big bay, Lola's big bay. So disembowel me, already!

I am walking back toward the barn, lugging Lola's saddle, which still has the girth affixed to one side. I will have to apologize to Marilee, of course, for getting the wrong horse, but I am thinking, Even when she apologizes back for treating me the way she treated me, I'm not sure I can forgive her.

Except that when I do get to the barn, it is worse. I see Lola's *bridle* just dumped on the ground in front of the horse's stall. Lola's bridle, which, similarly, costs a mint.

Anyway, this is the limit!

Marilee, you bitch! You have gone too far, I want to scream, but of course that would only get the horses upset—I mean the act of yelling, not the words, and so I just stand at the stall door and hiss at her, meanwhile fantasizing grabbing her by her long blond hair, which she is presently tucking up inside a hair net.

And then I have a twinge of pity. I mean, there she is, in her kind of yellowed white breeches wearing someone's cast-off coat. Her hunt cap looks as though it's been in use for a decade or more.

I mean, spit and polish, this girl ain't.

So I temper it. "What is it with you?" I say to her. "You are acting like a spoiled brat."

Marilee turns, her face still all contorted with

anger, and she clenches her teeth and says, "You just keep your hands off my horse."

Well.

I set the saddle down on some hay and I pick up the bridle and the longe line and I decide not even to deal with her again, not now, not ever. I will act as though nothing has happened, but when everybody is bad-mouthing her, though, I'm not going to butt in and say something nice, which I used to.

"Where's my whip?" I ask, because the long longe whip is gone.

Marilee ignores me.

I step into the stall next to hers, the stall with, I assume, *Lola's* big bay, and I bring him out. Fortunately he's clean, and I am about to tack him up, affix the longe line, and retrace my steps when— guess what?—Lola comes storming into the barn, leading the horse she had been riding.

She is red-faced, too. "Where were you?" she asks me, and points at the horse I've got. "Is he ready?"

"No, he's not ready," I scream at her, and her eyes whoosh wide open.

"Not ready?" she says. "Ro-bin, I ride in three minutes!"

"Well, maybe you need two grooms," I say as she grabs the saddle away from me and slings it up over the bay's back. All of this while she's still holding on to the other horse, the one she's just finished riding.

I take the other horse from her, which is the least I can do. Meanwhile, she's muttering something, probably about how hard it is to get decent help these days. And then she gives this big loud *tsk!*

Well, you know why. Because the bridle is filthy, and of course the saddle doesn't look too good either, both of them having been in the dirt. What is more, Lola now has a big ugly brown blob of a stain across the belly of the white breeches she is wearing.

I don't think she knows about the stain, and I'm sure not going to tell her.

She finishes tacking up and she moves off, and I lead the other horse out to where I can see what she's doing.

Lola is out there talking to the steward.

Well, okay, she's trying to reschedule her ride, and that makes sense. Because dressage shows aim at precision. If you're scheduled to go at, say, 2:32 or 1:06, you'd better be ready. But you can switch your ride with someone else—get it switched, that is—if some emergency like this, no time for warm-up, happens. Especially in Lo's case, because she's showing so many horses.

I see the steward nodding yes, and I see Lola smiling. I relax a little as Lo starts into the warm-up arena.

I continue walking the other horse, feeling his chest at intervals to make sure he's in fact cooling down, stealing a glance at Lo whenever I can.

Eventually, Marilee comes into the warm-up on the bay I'd mistakenly tacked up.

And all the anger that I've been storing is dissolved, changed, as if an alchemist of emotions had plied his trade, transforming my ire into something like awe.

The horse Marilee is on is about the same height

as Lo's, maybe 16.3, and marked the same way. They both have, as the expression goes, *lots of chrome*. Chrome is white, white markings, and they both have four white stockings and a big white blaze down their faces.

They don't move alike, though, and movement is what gets high scores in dressage. There's a whole separate category where the judge scores a horse for it. The horse that Lo was riding was maybe a six in the gaits department, but the horse that Marilee had! God, it was an eight, maybe even a nine.

What I mean is, the horse moved like—I don't know, a jungle cat maybe—big and loose and efficient, his legs stepping way way underneath his body to propel him forward, and his body itself all coiled energy ready to spring free.

Marilee, so tiny on his back, looked as though she belonged there. As though she'd spent her whole life waiting for this horse to come along.

Everyone else out there in the warm-up, Lola included, looked merely okay.

Not that there's anything wrong with okay. Okay is what I and, I daresay, the majority of riders, hope for.

Marilee's horse, though, had star quality, that indefinable presence that words alone can't convey. It's very much a, you'll-know-it-when-you-see-it kind of thing. I'm talking magnificent here.

I know, you're thinking, Doesn't my own horse, Spier, have it? I mean, after all, Spier was in the Olympics once. And you're right, he does, except that when this initial thing happened with Marilee,

I didn't have Spier yet, and so the only thing I could think of then was this:

One time Jeet and I were in the airport waiting for someone, and these men—these big, beautiful men—came waltzing through the terminal, en masse. I mean, they were larger than life, these men, and they even seemed to shine, as though some kind of light hovered around their bodies. And it turned out, they weren't ordinary men, they were the Dallas Cowboys, athletes, stars.

Anyway, Marilee's horse was like an equine Dallas Cowboy, a kind of primo specimen.

I remember Lo shouting, "How'm I doing?" and me looking at her for the first time.

"Oh, fine," I'd said. But I knew Marilee was going to sweep the class, maybe even sweep the whole show on the horse she was riding.

And Lo blew it anyway because she looked down at her breeches just before riding into the arena and freaked. She was so distraught about the brown goop that had somehow gotten all over her that I was surprised she remembered her test.

Even when she came out, instead of talking about her performance, she was talking about how her breeches were totally ruined by whatever it was and looking at me as if I were somehow to blame.

And I always cop to that right away, so I stood around feeling responsible. So it goes.

Marilee got a seventy-six on her test and Lola a sixty-something. A sixty-something is respectable, but a seventy-six, wow! After that, a lot of people tried to talk to Marilee, but she was uniformly rude to them, so that she was able to keep pretty much to herself, spectacular horse and all.

Lola, being in a fairly awful mood, kept me pretty busy, but I managed to go into the show office to ask who owned the horse Marilee was showing. The horse's name was Gentian and his breed was given as "grade," which means no breed at all, kind of a mongrel.

They said Marilee herself owned him.

I didn't believe them, of course, because Marilee was poorer than I was and horses like that just don't get bestowed on girls like Marilee no matter how well they ride. I also doubted that Gentian was no breed at all, although things like that do happen. It's a big gene pool and you don't *need* to be a fancy breed to show in dressage, or even win in dressage, for that matter. Still.

Then I thought: the boyfriend. God, where had she found an animal lover like that? As much as Jeet loves me, I can't imagine him in a bed full of dogs and cats, which is pretty much what I'm sure being with Marilee had to be like. Jeez. That Doberdane alone would take up half the bed. And those Chihuahuas. Instead of one big cold nose, you'd have all those little ones. Oy.

As you see, musing about Marilee's love life proved sufficiently distracting to get me through the rest of the show. I was only sorry that Lola was so mad at me, because it would have been fun if she'd been able to muse about it, too.

Anyway, the next day I thought I'd drop in on Marilee and give her a chance to make things up to me. And also, I admit it, I wanted to snoop. Maybe he'd be there, the boyfriend, and I could get to see what he looked like. Maybe he had animals of his own. A wombat, maybe, or a kangaroo. But at the very least, I'd get to see Marilee's super horse again.

I drove onto the property and up the long farm lane, and the cows she tended kept coming over to check me out. I'd inch on and they'd get out of the way, but the cows made me think fondly of Marilee again despite her behavior the day before.

Because Marilee could be pretty funny and one of her biggest jokes involved the cows.

She always drove out to feed them and so they always came to cars, but the thing is, she'd drive out honking, kind of as a bovine dinner bell.

Strangers of course would honk as soon as a cow appeared, and the next thing they knew, they'd be an island in a sea of cows, an island that couldn't budge.

Of course this drove most people to honk even more, honk longer, honk more frantically. Thus the cows would keep them and their vehicle absolutely gridlocked. It usually took about twenty minutes until the cows mooed around enough to figure out that the strange car they had surrounded wasn't the chuckwagon after all.

And Marilee would come out at that point and laugh her head off at the strangers.

See what I mean? She wasn't completely gone. Those who are completely gone—I mean of the women I've been describing, the unmarriageable ones—they don't have a sense of humor.

Anyway, as I neared Marilee's trailer, I could see the bay in the field beyond. He was walking, but even if I didn't know diddly about horses, I could see it was no ordinary walk. Out there in the field, he had long springy steps and an overreach—that is, his back legs reaching up beyond where his front legs had been—that was not to be believed.

I got out of the car and stood there, and Marilee came out and stood, too. Her yappy little Chihuahuas were with her, but they evidently were awed by the horse, too. They were milling around beside Marilee.

What did she see in dogs like that? Now, the Doberdane, who was big and friendly, I could understand.

I gestured toward the horse. "Gentian," I said. "That's a pretty name."

Marilee didn't answer.

"And he's a pretty horse, too," I went on. "Your ride yesterday was spectacular."

She still hadn't said a word. I looked over at her and she was eyeing me with something like suspicion.

"Jeez, Marilee," I said. "You may as well come clean. Because you know and I know that this isn't any ordinary horse, this is—"

She grabbed my forearm.

The Chihuahuas interpreted this as a sign that she was in danger. They came charging at my ankles, and I kicked out at them even as I pulled away from Marilee. "God," I said, about those pesky dogs, really, "this cannot go on!"

And then Marilee started to cry. "I knew we couldn't get away with it," she said.

Oh, God, I thought, Gentian is a stolen horse. That's the first thing that occurred to me. Then the next thing was, Well, she'll just have to give him back!

"You can't be blamed for wanting a horse like Gentian," I began, because that was certainly true. Then I thought, But if he were stolen, why would she take him to a horse show? That seemed pretty dumb.

She sniveled and hugged me and I patted her. "You might as well tell me," I said, and she nodded okay, she would.

I expected her to start with something about the new man in her life, but it never came up. Instead, she and I went into the pasture and she put a halter on Gentian and led him back into the barn.

He was a sweetheart, obviously suspecting a surprise meal or at least a treat of some kind. What he got, though, was Marilee rubbing at his belly with some kind of creamy stuff that looked like cold cream.

The color on his belly came off in a big brown stain on the towel that she'd used to wipe the creamy stuff off.

And there, on the horse's barrel, was a white mark shaped exactly like a spread-out hand. What was he, a Mafia horse? But they used a black hand, didn't they? And they weren't into horses, were they? Unless they'd branched out. I considered making jokes of this sort, but what with Marilee's solemnity, decided not to.

"What?" I asked her. "What does it mean?" The stain on the towel, I noted, was exactly the same as the stain all over Lola's white show breeches, too.

So inadvertently I *had* been responsible for it. The goop was probably all over the girth.

I repeated, "What does it mean?"

Marilee's mouth made an O and then she looked angry. "You tricked me," she said. "I thought you knew," she said. "I thought you figured it out."

"Figured what out?" I asked.

"Why do you think I was so mad?" she asked me. "I'd just put this stuff on him," she continued, holding up a bottle of something for me to see. "And you came along and tacked him up. I thought, Oh, shit! It's going to rub right off."

I stared blindly in response.

"Oh, Jesus, Robin, you don't know a damn thing," she said, opening the bottle and pulling out a dauber and then rubbing some kind of dark liquid over the whole white hand mark, making it brown. "I never should have told you. Now," she said, "I really will be in trouble."

"With who?" I tried. "With your boyfriend?"

"I don't have any boyfriend," she said.

I followed her and Gentian back out to the pasture. "Well, I heard you had," I said. "And I'll bet he's the one that got you mixed up in this." Whatever it was.

She grabbed my hand and she looked at me with her eyes all wet and shining. "Robin," she said, "if you don't want me to get hurt and if you don't want to get hurt yourself, get out of here. Forget that I ever showed you this. Just drop it. Just leave me alone."

A lot of people think I'm dense, but I ask you— could you have figured out whatever was going on here? Of course not. And I can tell when I'm not wanted, too.

"Fine," I said, "I'll do that."

She turned Gentian loose and looked at me hard. "I'm not kidding, Robin," she said. "My life is at stake here. You have to promise me that you won't say a word about this to anybody."

"Okay," I said. "I promise." I was thinking she was whacko. I mean, that happens when you're alone too much, you get weirder and weirder because there's no one there to point out that the weirdnesses are accumulating. So maybe there wasn't any boyfriend after all.

So I kept my promise and didn't tell anyone, not even Jeet or Lola, and then the next competition came and this time Marilee and Gentian didn't show up, which was odd since they'd entered and paid their entry fees and stabling and stuff.

That prompted everyone to talk about the horse. One person said the horse put him in mind of the famous German stallion Sturmgeist.

Everyone—even people who had never heard of Sturmgeist, like me—said oh, yes, yes indeed he did.

I thought, Hmmm.

Next day I dropped in on Len Reasoner, my vet. He was out behind the main building, and he had a mare in the stocks. He was wearing rubber gloves and an apron and he was carrying what looked like a drinking straw. "Howdy." He smiled at me.

"Can odd markings, like birthmarks, be genetically transmitted from horse to horse?" I asked.

"Whoa," he said. "Didn't your mama ever tell you that first you say, 'Hi, how are you?' and then you kind of ease off in the direction that you want the conversation to take?"

"But—"

"Come on, now. 'Hi, how are you?' "

"Hi, how are you," I said. "But can birthmarks pass on from one generation to the next and do you know of any horse that has a hand-shaped thing"—I indicated my belly—"like right here?"

"I'm fine, little lady," he said. "And how are you?"

"Fine, fine. But can they? Birthmarks? And do you? I mean, know of any horse with one like that?"

He sighed in a resigned sort of way. "They probably can be passed on," he said, "and no, I don't know of any. Now, is that it for you today, missie, or am I gonna have you hanging around while I inseminate this mare?"

"That's it."

"You might try A&M," he suggested.

He meant Texas A&M, which had a vet school. Except that it was in College Station, which was like an hour and a half away. "Would they let me use their library?" I asked.

"Don't see why not, you being so charming and all."

Did he mean I wasn't?

"But they'd let *you*, wouldn't they? I mean, didn't you graduate from A&M?"

"Oh, they'd let me. And I could go down there and do it while you inseminate *this* mare and those other mares out yonder. Sounds like a good trade to me, spending my day in the library down at A&M while you're up to your elbows here. Of course, my clients might not like it, you not being trained as a vet and all, but—"

"Okay, okay, I get it," I interrupted him. He had, as usual, made his point.

"There's somebody down in LaGrange," he said. "Kent something. I think he knows a little bit about breeding. Has some pricey mare from overseas."

"Is he Marilee Hart's boyfriend?" I asked.

But I guess he wasn't, because Len said, "Marilee Hart has a boyfriend?"

I drove to Marilee's trailer again then, only to find that Marilee wasn't at home. Her truck and horse trailer were gone, too. There was nothing, no movement at all, which was strange, but hey.

I had the sense, though, that it was too quiet, if you know what I mean. Sure enough, I stopped over there four or five times in the next two days and there wasn't any change. Someone had evidently been feeding the cows, though.

I looked in Marilee's mailbox. Stuff, mostly junk, had piled up in there.

I called the sheriff and reported Marilee missing. He didn't seem upset. In fact, when it turned out that I knew next to nothing about her, he was downright bored. I don't even think he wrote down what I told him.

In fact, everyone was bored. I couldn't get a soul to listen to me—not Jeet, not Lola—when I talked about Marilee being gone.

Over the next few weeks, I kept checking her mailbox, and she kept getting mail that hadn't been picked up. Some of the mail was from the vet's office, too. Bills for the board of the Chihuahuas were way overdue, no doubt.

I went back to his office. "Len," I said, "about Marilee Hart's Chihuahuas."

"What about them?" Len said.

"You've been billing her and—"

"Robin, Robin, Robin," he said. "Have you been going through that girl's mail?"

"Well, yes, but—"

"Didn't your mama ever tell you that going through someone's mail is a federal offense?"

"Well, no, but—"

"What are we going to do with you?" he said, shaking his head.

"Well anyway, she's way overdue and—"

"Her dogs have been taken care of," he said.

I froze. "Oh, God," I said. "You mean doggie heaven."

"Doggie heaven?" he repeated. Then, to my relief, he said, "No, I don't mean doggie heaven, I mean somebody came for them, paid the bill, and carted them off. All six of the little suckers and the Doberdane, too."

"You mean took them to Marilee?"

"No, I mean adopted them. After sixty days, we give up on people, and that's what I did. I gave up on Marilee."

"Somebody adopted those Chihuahuas?" I asked.
"Someone actually wanted them?"

He laughed. "Takes all kinds," he said.

Eventually I did make my way down to A&M,
where I did find a picture of the stallion Sturmgeist. He was standing with his off side—his right
side, that is—to the camera, his groom at his head.
So the birthmark—if he had such a one—was not
visible, nor did it appear to be mentioned in the
text.

I say "appear to be" because the text was in German. Not that I speak German, but the text had all
the same words in it that the other horses' blurbs
had, and I assume the word for birthmark would
thus have stood out.

On Gentian the mark had been on the near
side—the left side—of the belly. Or I guess I should
say barrel, which is more correct, more dignified.

I trundled the volume over to a coin-operated
photocopy machine and for twenty-five cents made
a print of the page. Despite the exorbitant cost, it
was a terrible print, all black and white with no intervening gray. Still, it just might come in handy.

Then—and this was my final bid in the Marilee
Hart department—I made one last pass at her
trailer.

Until then, I hadn't gone inside, but now I sort of
heaved myself against the door until it gave way.
Once in there, I was a hundred percent convinced
that something was awry because all of Marilee's
trophies and ribbons were there.

She appeared to have won plenty. The ribbons

were blue, but age had purpled them. The silver on
the trophies had gone brown. I remember having
this twinge of is-this-all-there-is? A moment when I
wondered, kind of morbidly, what would be left of
me when I was gone.

And then I shrugged it off, went back to my
truck, drove home, and tried to get it out of my
mind.

One more shot, I thought. I tried the sheriff
again, even saying that there were rumors about a
mysterious boyfriend, but to no avail.

And so I did as everyone advised and forgot
about Marilee Hart completely.

Until I'd come face to face again with her in Mexico right now.

CHAPTER 4

"So you see," I said, having relayed to Marilee pretty much all that I've relayed to you, "I haven't been searching per se. Still, it is pretty cool, running into you like this."

She didn't look as though she agreed.

"Well," I babbled on, "*I* think it is."

Except for her hair, which was bobbed at chin level in a way that looked expensive, she seemed pretty much the same. "I like your hair, too," I tried, hoping to ignite some spark of human feeling. Because the shotgun was still very much at her side.

"Ro-bin," she said, breaking my name into separate syllables the way everyone since my mother does when they're exasperated with me.

"What?" I asked her.

"Oh, never mind," she said. "It probably *is* an accident, you being here. It would be just my luck."

She looked glum.

I don't even know how I was going to respond, because all of a sudden I was seized by the most powerful bathroom urge—I'm talking number two here—that I've ever had in my life. I mean, I was practically doubled over by it, and I was terrified by its intensity.

I ran past Marilee, shotgun and all, and continued up the road, the Chihuahuas swarming around me as I did so. There was a sort of hill ahead, and I thought if I could just get over it and get my pants down, I'd be fine.

"Robin, stop!" Marilee shouted, and the Chihuahuas went into a yapping frenzy.

"I have to use your bathroom," I screamed, spying a white stucco—God, I don't know, mansion!—beyond the hill and now beelining for it.

"Robin, you can't, you . . ." I think she knew her protests were useless.

I heard her running behind me, but I didn't care. God. I was just sure I would totally disgrace myself right then and there.

I was at the big double set of doors now. I pushed and they gave way.

"Third door on the right," Marilee was yelling behind me.

Oh.

I slammed the door behind me, yanked everything down, and hurled myself into position at the toilet bowl, and just in the absolute nick of time. I was doubled over with cramps that felt like blows. I don't know how long all this lasted, really, but it seemed I went and went and went, went so much that my hands were shaking and my forehead was beading with sweat. I thought I would die right there on Marilee's toilet.

Three of the dogs had made it into the tiny enclosure with me, but they had the sense to leave me alone. In fact, they hovered at the door, whining to be released.

Ha! I thought.

Served the little boogers right.

Someone—Marilee, I guess—opened the door and let them out, then quickly slammed it shut again.

I was too sick and spent to be embarrassed.

Marilee talked to me through the door. "Did you drink any tap water?" she asked.

"I'm not sure."

"How," she said, "can you not be sure?"

Well, I had gone into an ice-cream parlor the day Jeet and I had arrived, and after my ice cream, I had asked, as told, for *agua mineral*. The people there said they only had *agua natural*. I didn't exactly drink it, but I didn't want to hurt their feelings, so I kind of bumped it up against my lips and pretended to be drinking it.

I told her that.

She said that was probably enough to do it.

Her concern made me think our friendship had been restored, but that wasn't the case. When I emerged, Marilee still had the gun. "You okay?" she asked, kind of contradictorily.

"No."

"It's *turista*," she explained. "Better get to a *farmacia* and get some medicine. They have stuff that's supposed to help."

I'd recovered enough to look around.

The building, though beautiful, wasn't even the house. It was a stable, and on a par with Hans Bell's place, stucco and timber with elaborately

curlicued wrought-iron trim. "Do you live here or
work here or what?" I asked.

Marilee looked, for a fleeting instant, boastful. "I
live here," she said. "Yes."

"In an apartment or what?" I sized the place up.
Actually, even one of the stalls would have been
nicer than that trailer she'd abandoned.

"No, Robin, in the manor house. I am"—she
paused here, as if she didn't know what to say—"in
charge," she decided.

So she wasn't the owner, I figured. But still.

"But how did you wangle it?" I asked. Then I
thought, inexplicably, of Len Reasoner, my vet, saying, "Didn't your mama tell you not to ask imperti-
nent questions and expect any answers?" and I
softened it by saying, "I'm doing a story on your
breeding operation for *Horse Play*. That's why I
need to know."

Marilee lifted the gun menacingly yet again.
"Like hell you are," she said. "I can't believe you've
got me talking to you like this. Now get out of here.
And don't you dare tell anybody that you saw me
here. Don't tell anybody anything."

"Tell anybody what? Did you take that horse with
the handprint with you when you left?" I asked.

"Oh, God, Robin, you are so . . ."

I didn't get to hear what she thought I was, because my *turista* kicked in again. I ran back to the
little bathroom and picked up where I'd left off.

Meanwhile, Marilee stood outside the door telling
me that I had to leave the minute I was done.
Leave and never come back.

Well. When you're sitting on a toilet in a strange

stable in a foreign country and a woman you haven't seen for three years is threatening you with a sawed-off shotgun, you'll agree to anything.

I came out of the bathroom in a weakened state. I had picked up a box of tissues. "Just in case," I said.

She actually smiled. "Okay," she said. "But Robin, promise me you'll keep your mouth shut."

Yeah, yeah, yeah. "I promise," I said.

I led the way outside and she sort of hung back a little, urging me along the sandy road. I didn't like myself for it, but I wanted to part friends, so I tried to converse.

"Your hair really does look cute that way," I told her. "Do they do that here? I mean, in San Miguel?" It looked pretty high fashion for a little colonial town. Of course, with all the tourists, I guess it was possible there would be a place. I mean, even Jackie O was said to have come here.

"I get it done in Mexico," she said.

I guess I looked puzzled. San Miguel, after all, was Mexico. So she explained: "Mexico City."

"Ah."

We had reached the little Fiesta.

"Do you still have Plum?" she asked me, meaning the mare I'd bought off the track.

"You bet."

"And how about Mother?" Meaning my ancient Dodge truck.

"Mother, too."

"Good."

"Marilee." I couldn't help bragging. "I actually

have a Grand Prix horse now. An old one, retired."
And I told her all about Spier.

This did engage her interest, and we did maybe
five minutes on the value of schoolmasters—that is,
old horses who've been well trained and who can
thus impart knowledge to riders who aren't that far
along.

Of course I didn't linger on the bad-news part of
having a horse who knew so much, which is that
every little breath means something to them. In my
own case, I found out I was doing an incredible
amount of unintentional moving around. Poor
Spier.

But the point is, when I got back into the car, we
were as close to being buddies as we ever were. I
turned the car around and waved. She stood, her
Chihuahuas swirling around at her feet, watching
me go. Good for her, I thought. She'd lucked out.
Maybe she'd come here with the boyfriend, too. The
one she'd pretended didn't exist.

And I guess that would have been the end of it if
I hadn't passed an old Jaguar roadster going in the
opposite direction. An old Jaguar driven by someone who looked mighty familiar to me.

Well, maybe not *mighty* familiar, but some.

It had been three years, and my view of him had
been brief, but still . . . I could have sworn the
driver was the groom, the man who, in the picture
I'd seen, had stood next to Sturmgeist. Sturmgeist's
groom.

Whoa. If *he* had been the elusive boyfriend,

things were starting to add up. Except that math isn't one of my strong points.

In any case, I made a U-turn and tried to catch up to him so that I could see whether he turned in where I had, but he didn't. I could see him up ahead and knew that he'd driven right past the road that led into the golden hill. And anyway, how could it have been otherwise? I mean, if I couldn't get a Fiesta up that road, how would he do it in a Jaguar?

I U-turned back again, toward town.

Then I thought, well maybe he had seen me as he passed and therefore had driven past the road on purpose, except that I knew it wasn't so. One of the main reasons I'd recognized him was the straight-ahead, no-nonsense expression he'd worn on his face, the same expression he'd had in the photograph.

Could he have stolen Sturmgeist?

No. If a horse like that had been stolen three years before, there would have been some outcry, some word of it, some alarm. And anyway, hadn't I more or less checked out the stolen-horse angle when I'd first started looking into Marilee's disappearance?

Well, not in depth, but some.

But what then?

The obvious conclusion was that I didn't remember this guy in the Jag at all. That my hyperactive mind was at it again. I tried to convince myself that such was the case, but I wasn't having any luck at all.

In fact, I formed a contrary notion with some de-

gree of certainty, to wit: The horse and the guy in
the Jag and Marilee Hart's newfound fortune were
somehow intimately bound.

How could I let a thing like this go? I mean, I
was a reporter now, right? It was my job. And I was
a natural reporter, too, because my bones were
singing that *here*, right here, was a story!

So I did another U and sped up to around eighty.
When I came to a long straightaway, the Jag was
nowhere in sight. So either he *had* turned in somewhere or he had yielded to the same temptation I
had, to speed.

If that's what, then I might as well give it up. I
was not going to catch a Jaguar with the car I was
driving. Also, a Mexican patrolman might well
catch me. So I turned again toward San Miguel and
drove like the proverbial little old lady from Pasa-
dena. A little old lady who, deep down, had the
combined instincts of Kinsey Millhone and Sam
Spade.

CHAPTER 5

"You are imagining things," Jeet was saying. I had just unspooled the entire tale for his benefit. I expected him to ooh and aah and say, "I'd give my eyeteeth for a story like this one," but instead he was back to finger wagging.

"I should have known better than to turn you loose in a foreign country," he said, "for an entire day. It's a miracle you weren't arrested, barging in on people like that."

"But it wasn't people, Jeet. It was Marilee. Marilee, who disappeared . . ."

But try as I might, I couldn't even get to the part about the boyfriend in the Jag.

"You can tell me later," Jeet said. "Right now I want you to go through your things and make sure you have something really special to wear tonight. Because tonight"—his eyes lit up—"tonight, we are running with the big dogs."

Jeet doesn't usually talk this way. Plus I didn't want to run with dogs of any size, not after those Chihuahuas.

And I was sick, too. I'd actually had to *use* the

61

tissues I'd taken from Marilee's on my way back to
the hotel.

I would have to, as Marilee suggested, get myself
to a *farmacia*. But I didn't want Jeet to know about
my plight and then have to tell him about pretending to drink the *agua natural*. This would only
spark another lecture.

But at that particular point, I probably could
have left the room and locked myself in the john for
fifteen minutes before he'd have noticed I was gone,
because he was off and running, extremely pleased
with himself.

"Ernesto Quinto," Jeet was saying. "Ernesto
Quinto, the world-famous gourmet! Ernesto Quinto
has invited us to his *home*."

I figured that Ernesto Quinto must be a pretty
big deal. I mean, Jeet and I once got to eat at the
governor's mansion back in Texas and he hadn't
carried on like this.

"He's actually a diplomat," Jeet was telling me.
"And rich. And he flies in all kinds of goodies for
his dinner parties. I've read about them in magazines. Truffles, Dungeness crab, sourdough bread
from San Francisco . . ."

"Like Frank Sinatra," I said.

That stopped him. "Like Frank Sinatra, yes." But
he recovered. "So go on, look through your things,"
he told me. "You might actually have to buy something."

Buy something! This Quinto guy must be the cul-
inary equivalent of the pope. It made me stubborn,
somehow. "I have a dress," I said. "Basic black. It'll

be fine." It's what I call the Standard Fat Girl's Outfit, but hey, it works.

"Did you bring that shawl thing you have." He gestured as if wrapping himself in a winding sheet. "That turquoise one with the fringe?"

I smiled at him. "Yeah."

"You look great in that," he said, about to put his arms around me.

Except that my *turista* made yet another appearance, sudden and unbidden, as *turista* is wont to do. I shoved Jeet aside as if he were a would-be attacker and headed toward the bathroom, where, even though we'd been married forever, I hated thinking about all that Jeet was about to hear.

In fact, our whole floor could probably hear. Think Fourth of July here.

I wondered if maybe we could change hotels.

When I came out, of course, Jeet wasn't even minimally amorous anymore. He asked—and considering how thrilled he had been about the invite, you know what a huge deal this was—if maybe we shouldn't bow out of the dinner with Ernesto Quinto.

"I'll be fine," I assured him, sounding far more convinced than I felt. "I'm going out to a drugstore to get something for it. And if it doesn't work, you can go without me. Okay?"

"Okay."

I thus escaped into the street without being grilled about what sort of water I'd had to drink.

Even though San Miguel has a lot of English-speaking folk wandering through it, there are still some staunch Spanish-only speakers about.

Such as the three clerks inside the *farmacia* I'd selected, solemn-faced women with deep-lined serious faces.

I'd said, "Excuse me, but do you—" only to be interrupted with a firm chorus of, *"No inglés."*

Maybe I ought to have walked out, gone to another place, but I didn't. What I figured was, it's their country, right? Except that my phrase book didn't include anything beyond *Estoy enfermo,* "I am sick," which was way too general to score me anything of value.

"Kaopectate?" I tried.

The three clerks looked at each other and then made elaborate shrugging gestures at me.

I tried pantomime. I pretended to be walking in the door, very casually. Then I grabbed my belly, as if hit by an enormous cramp. I ran like mad toward the corner of the store—the bathroom in my skit—and slammed an imaginary door behind me. I looked over at them. They were waiting, but something in their expression had softened.

I thought, Aha! I'm making progress here. And thank God. I mean, I didn't want to have to descend to the level of a second grader and start making fart noises, right?

I guess they'd never seen an American—or for all I know, anyone of any nationality—behave this way. The corners of their mouths went up reluctantly. And once that had happened, audible sounds of merriment came issuing from their mouths.

Ladies and gentlemen, I had won their hearts. I felt as though I ought to segue into a Sally Fields, you-like-me-you-really-like-me kind of speech, though I didn't.

They were still laughing as one of them placed a quart-sized bottle on the counter for me. Still, I wanted to know what my malady, in Spanish, might be called. *"Como se llama este enfermo?"* I tried. It was like a game show, *Name That Disease*.

"Diarrea," the clerks chorused.

"Diarrea?" It sounded exactly like our word for it. So I'd made a total fool of myself almost for nothing.

One of the clerks held up a spoon in one hand, three fingers with another. So, I was supposed to take a spoonful every three hours.

"Uno"—I pointed at the spoon—*"por tres horas?"* just to confirm.

"No, no."

"Tres," I tried, pointing at the fingers, followed by "spoonfuls," pointing at the spoon.

"Sí."

Three spoonfuls. But every . . . what? Every hour? I mimed taking one, then said, *"Una hora,"* mimed taking another, said *"Una hora"* again. Did a third and was about to start on number four when two of the three interrupted with a "No."

"Por día," one said.

Okay. Three spoonfuls a day.

Then I bid them *gracias* and was out of there.

The thing about diarrhea is that you always think each time you've gone is the last time. I mean, it has to be, right? And then it never is.

But I was in that state of thinking that the malady perhaps was done with me, and so I behaved, not like a sick person, but like a tourist.

I walked up to the park in the center of town—the Jardín, they call it. It's the place where tourists meet and greet, yes, but where locals hang out as well. There are tall trees and rows of benches, and there's a bandstand in the midst of them.

The Parroquia, a beautiful baroque church, fronts one side of the square, while assorted restaurants, gift shops, and art galleries take charge of the other three.

There are panhandlers. There are boys offering shoeshines. There are vendors selling trinkets and food. There are gaggles of Mexican schoolchildren in various uniforms, like girls in jumpers and blouses or pleated skirts and blazers and boys in little coats and ties.

And fortunately for me, it turns out, there's a *sanitario*—a public toilet. I all but trampled twelve small children who were smiling at me, in order to get there.

I threw the peso that the facility cost at the attendant, who was probably used to this. But maybe not, because the tiny wad of toilet paper he gave me in exchange, let me tell you, wasn't enough. By the time I left, I'd used the remaining facial tissue, and I thanked whatever god was in charge of my particular affliction that I had it with me to use.

The attendant was a real gallant at the last, too, and averted his eyes as I left. Outside, I remembered the medicine and drank some right from the bottle.

Talk about potent! I could feel that amber liquid

tying a square knot in my lower bowel as I walked back to the hotel.

I was going to be fine tonight at Ernesto Quinto's. This medicine would see to it.

When I rounded the corner I encountered an impromptu parade. Two pickup trucks drove by, each decorated with orange, white, and green plastic banners, and each bearing in the truck bed a motorcycle mounted by a pretty Mexican teenage girl. The San Miguel police, in the little Volkswagen bugs that they drive, headed up the front and brought up the rear.

What a wonderful country. Despite the water, I mean.

When I got back to the hotel there was a commotion in the lobby. My husband was smack in the center of it. There were flashbulbs popping and someone with a video camera was going to town.

In broken English, an interviewer was asking Jeet his impressions of Mexican cuisine.

Jeet was beaming, talking about the freshness of the fruit and vegetables.

Ah, sí, muy fresca, the interviewer said, showing off his knowledge of *inglés.*

I know what you're thinking. You're thinking, Wouldn't you get *turista* from those? But the fact is, if whoever's preparing it (a) doesn't handle money, and (b) peels the stuff, you're okay.

I could hire myself out as a *turista* consultant.

I'd have hung around but I didn't see anything resembling a public rest room on that floor. So I played it safe and went upstairs to our room.

* * *

I pondered taking the medicine with me to Ernesto Quinto's that night, and finally hit upon the idea of rinsing out those tiny liquor bottles and putting some of the stuff in them. Our room had included several in a little welcome basket when we arrived. The whole basket was still intact. I poked through the cellophane, dumped the Scotch and sherry and gin in the sink, scrubbed the labels off the bottles and the caps, and began the process of transference.

I had just tucked one of the tiny bottles into my evening bag when Jeet returned.

"Hey," I said, "you're a celebrity."

He blushed a bit.

"It's great," I told him. "You deserve it."

"It is kind of fun."

"How'd they hear about you?" I asked.

"I don't know."

"Come to think of it," I went on, "how did Ernesto Quinto hear?"

Before Jeet could answer, there was a bloodcurdling shriek. It was followed by a second, then a third. Jeet and I ran out into the hall.

There was a man lying there, a machete handle sticking up from the center of his back, the blade, presumably below it.

The stabbing must have just happened, too, because the blood—a growing bright red band around the hilt—was only beginning to show.

The screamers were women who had happened upon whoever it was.

And whoever it was still had his leather apron on.

I knew without seeing the front of him that it was the blacksmith, Felipe.

"Jeet," I whispered, pulling him back inside our room.

"I know, I know, it's awful," he said, wrapping himself around me.

"It's worse than that," I said, about to tell him that I knew who the dead guy was.

Except, would the Mexican police believe that, yes, I'd met the victim that very day, but I didn't have anything to do with his death. And that no matter how it looked, he couldn't have been coming to see me.

They wouldn't buy it for a minute.

And I'd end up just the way Jeet feared I would: in a Mexican jail.

"What were you going to say?" Jeet asked.

"Uh, who? Me?"

CHAPTER 6

Several minutes had elapsed without the hubbub in the hallway abating.

And Jeet was whispering, "Oh, God. I can't imagine calling Ernesto and telling him we can't come because there's a body right outside our door. But I know, Robin, that if we go out there, it'll be a big mistake."

"You're right," I said. "But won't they eventually ask us, you know, if we heard anything?"

"I don't know. We didn't. I mean, except for the screaming."

That was true.

"Poor guy. I wonder who he was."

I was tempted again to tell Jeet, but I didn't.

"Maybe I should call," he said.

"Jeet," I reminded him. "There's no phone in here." Phones weren't that common in San Miguel. I mean, we had hot water night and day. Wasn't that enough in the way of amenities? I would have said that to Jeet, kind of to lighten things up, but right then they knocked on our door.

"*Policía,*" a male voice said.

Jeet opened it. "Yes?"

It was probably obvious to the police that Jeet already knew about the body. I mean, otherwise, wouldn't he have expressed some surprise? Instead, he was acting offhand. As though the cop had stepped over the corpse to sell raffle tickets or something.

"You are Robin Vaughan?" the policeman asked him, first introducing himself as Ramon Pedras. He was wearing an odd kind of uniform, and instead of a gun, he had, I swear, a screwdriver tucked into a little holster.

Jeet didn't seem to notice the officer's weapon. He turned and stared at me. He finally had something appropriate on his face—a startled expression, which, I'm sure, mirrored my own. I guess because of what he'd just been asked. There was no way around it.

Pedras looked past Jeet now at me. "Ah," he said, moving into the room. "*You* are Robin Vaughan. *Señora* Robin Vaughan." His English was heavily accented, but otherwise just fine.

"Yes," I said.

Officer Pedras stepped aside and gestured at Felipe, who was now face down on a stretcher. "We have had a little unpleasantness, señora. And the unfortunate victim had with him this," he said, holding up a little slip of paper.

"What is it?" Jeet asked, stepping toward him.

I came closer, too, in order to peer.

It was written in pencil. My name. Followed by the name of the hotel.

"Look. I met him once," I said, "this afternoon. He didn't even know me, really. I mean, I told him my whole name, but I don't know his name, except for the first name, Felipe. I mean—"

"His name is Felipe?" Pedras asked.

"Yes."

"How very interesting that you know that, señora, when you have not even seen his face."

"What do you mean?"

"He is face down on the stretcher," Pedras pointed out. "And he was face down when the bit of unpleasantness overtook him."

I can't explain how I knew this, but Pedras seemed to be teasing rather than accusing me. There was something flirty about it, so I wasn't inclined to panic. But maybe that was just his investigative technique.

I gestured toward the hallway. "Well, he's wearing that apron," I said. "That blacksmith's apron. Felipe was a blacksmith."

"Hmmm," the officer said, weighing my words. "That could be." Then he waved me out into the hall. "All right," he said. "Come look at this man's face. Just to be sure."

It was Felipe, all right, his features frozen into rude surprise.

"Can you tell me what it is that he might want to see you about?" Pedras asked. "A reason?"

"I really can't," I said. Maybe he wondered if I'd found Milagro. Except that he really would have had to dig in order to come up with the name of my hotel. I doubt that his curiosity about a breeding farm had been that strong. So it was probably something else. Something unrelated.

"It is curious in the extreme," Officer Pedras allowed. He was looking at me in that flirty way of his.

And actually, he was kind of cute. In a Jimmy Smits sort of way. Well, I guess that means more than kind of. All *right*, he was gorgeous. But as a happily married woman, I attempted not to notice, okay?

"Maybe we should get in touch with the American embassy," Jeet was saying. His brow was furrowed, as if he were genuinely worried.

"Call Ernesto Quinto," I suggested. I actually meant about dinner, about how we weren't going to be able to be there after all. The police officer, however, took it otherwise.

"My apologies," he said. "That will not be necessary." Then he looked at me in my basic black dress for the first time. I mean, really looked. "You are going to dinner with Señor Quinto, sí? Very well. Have your dinner, and come to my office in the morning. Is that agreeable?"

"Very," Jeet said.

"Good. The *federales* have been notified and they will join us then."

"Very good," Jeet said, sounding calm as could be.

But when we closed the door to the room behind us, Jeet was in a state of panic. "The *federales*! Let's get out of here. Out of Mexico. Let's leave right now. Let's—"

A knock.

It was our policeman. "You will of course remain in San Miguel."

Jeet composed himself and said, softly, "Of course."

"Very good."

But then Jeet shut the door and went ballistic—or what is the expression now? went *postal*—yet again. "If we drive all night," he was saying, gesticulating wildly and pacing about, "we could be back in the States in ten, maybe twelve hours. We could—"

"We can't do that," I said. It was like role reversal or something. "For one thing, driving in Mexico at night is dangerous." And it is, because there are animals—oxen, horses, burros, cows—who roam the highways. A head-on with an ox? I'd risk the *federales* any day.

"Oh God." Jeet sat on the bed and buried his face in his hands.

I wanted to tell him it would be okay. I mean, the head cop liked me, didn't he? But I didn't think this would calm Jeet necessarily. It would merely turn his anxiety in another direction.

"Jeet, listen," I said, crouching beside him. "If Ernesto Quinto is so powerful, then let's tell him what happened and get him to help us. I mean, surely you don't think they think I murdered this man."

"I don't know, I just don't know."

"Well, I do know," I said. "I am not a murderer. No jury is going to believe that I'm a murderer."

"Maybe they don't *have* juries," he said.

"Look," I said. "Let's get the Fiesta and boogie over to Ernesto's." I reached past him and grabbed my shawl. "Now come on."

Ernesto Quinto was unctuous, but inasmuch as he assured us that he would take care of everything, I managed to get past it. "Eat," he enjoined us, "drink, and be merry." It's my guess that he didn't know how that quotation ends.

But still, I didn't want to spend the rest of my life thinking about the corpse of poor Felipe. I mean, I barely knew the man. It was just an odd coincidence, right?

Right.

I glugged a glass of something sweet and tried to smile. For a while it worked. I even, for a while, got into touring Ernesto's house, which was at the outer edge of San Miguel, cantilevered over an unpopulated canyon, a kind of Mexican version of Frank Lloyd Wright's Fallingwater.

On one of the levels, there was a telescope mounted on a tripod. "What do you see out there?" I asked.

Ernesto sort of smirked. "Wild game," he said.

"Like what?" I wondered. Bad mistake.

Ernesto delighted in telling me. "It is—how do you say it—a lovers' lane, the ridge over there," he said, and winked.

Yuk.

Not yuk to a lovers' lane, you understand. Yuk to the sort of man who would use a telescope to spy on the lovers. Or admit that he did to two virtual strangers. It was tantamount to, I don't know, something out of *Eating Raoul*.

I gave Jeet a meaningful look, one of those can-you-believe-it? glances that sometimes pass between husband and wife, but mine went unnoticed. Jeet was looking not at me but at our host. Clearly, Jeet wasn't seeing him as an overweight lecher, as

I was, but as—I don't know what? A fellow gourmet. A man who—as Jeet would undoubtedly put it later—knew how to live graciously.

Jeet would probably go on and on about Ernesto Quinto's place, too. It was all timbered ceilings and Saltillo tile floors and glass with copper accents, an extreme show of wealth. I mean, we are talking *Architectural Digest* here. Think utter magnificence, all right? Mexican, yes, but ultramodern, too.

In fact, the section where Ernesto lived was brand-new, an unplanned expansion of the city of San Miguel, I guessed.

Because the nice houses ended and the places we'd passed immediately before reaching Ernesto's were hovels—tin rooves over cardboard, practically, which served as homes for the peasants. There was something ugly in building *this* so close to *that*.

Except that they'd have been leveled, the hovels, in most other countries. Here, at least, the developers, if that was what they were, had hopscotched over the poorer neighborhood.

Still.

Of course, it's easy for me to say this since I'm not and never have been fabulously wealthy. Or even minorly wealthy. I mean, who knows, I might turn into a real let-them-eat-cake type given half a chance.

And besides, if Ernesto could keep me out of a Mexican slammer, I shouldn't be so critical of his lifestyle. In fact, I should be in his thrall.

"Everything the best," Ernesto was saying, and Jeet was beaming up at him, impressed, I could tell. "I slaughter my own cows," Ernesto boasted, and my stomach turned. "I have a freezer full of the finest down those stairs." He pointed at a wide staircase ahead of us. "I will show you."

"No, thanks." I'd seen enough in the way of carcasses for the day.

But there was one more carcass yet to come.

Two servants brought it to the table, still on its spit, as our third and possibly main course. It was a pig, roasted, with cherries in its eyes and an apple in its mouth. Just like in the movies about Rome right before the fall.

Jeet was in heaven.

Me, I took one look at the pig and it and Jeet both dissolved in waves as I passed out, *thump*, on the cold, tile floor.

I came to in an upstairs bedroom, Jeet, Ernesto, and a maid in a stiff little uniform hovering over me. "The doctor is tied up, Ernesto says, but as soon as he can, he'll be here," Jeet said.

"I'm okay," I said. "It was the pig. I just . . ." I just don't like seeing animals that way. And it's hypocritical on my part, too, because I can eat ground beef just fine. It's when anything looks like an animal part—like a shoulder or a rump or even in the case of chickens, a breast or a thigh—that I wilt like this. And *this*—the whole animal being presented that way—was particularly gross and disgusting, maybe more so because I'd been so delighted, not all that many hours ago, to see a pig sleeping on a doorstep much the way a Collie might in the States. I don't know, call me sentimental.

"I think," Jeet said, his hand cool on my forehead, "it was just . . . the weight of the day." It sounded like a Merchant-Ivory film or something, *The Weight of the Day*, starring Anthony Hopkins as a repressed trainer.

"How long was I out?" I asked him, blinking.

"Not long."

"Well, go on and eat your pig," I said, "I'll be fine."

I don't impose my dietary peculiarities on my spouse. In fact, if I tried to, he would probably lose his job, since reviewing meals in restaurants, most of which serve meat, is what he does, mostly. Oh, he's working on a book, too, but isn't everyone? Mainly he does what we were here in Mexico to do: evaluate the cuisine.

"Ernesto has invited us to move in here with him for the rest of our stay," Jeet said.

I sat bolt upright. "No," I said ungraciously. "No." And just as Ernesto appeared at Jeet's shoulder.

"She's not herself at all," Jeet apologized for me.

"It's understandable," Ernesto told him. "I am not offended."

"Robin, it makes good sense. We cannot stay in a hotel where people are being murdered in the halls. And you shouldn't get out of bed tonight at all."

"Why?" I demanded. "Why shouldn't I?"

"Because you're sick," he said. "And because the doctor is on his way. Now listen to me," he said, looking very serious. "I am going to the hotel room to gather up our things. I'll be back."

"Jeet, no," I said. I don't know what my problem with this was, but I had one. Call it intuition, I don't know. All I could think of was *Gaslight*, that old movie where Ingrid Bergman gets sicker and sicker upstairs in that old house. I think it was Ingrid Bergman. Anyway, I was sure that if I stayed, it would be me.

I mean, there were women who didn't go off with Ted Bundy. They had followed their intuition. Well, I was doing that, too.

Not that I thought Ernesto was a serial killer. I just didn't like him, and hey, I'm entitled.

"I will wait with her," Ernesto said.

"Thank you, my friend," Jeet responded.

Great.

Jeet wasn't ten minutes out the door when I felt a familiar pressure, though slight, in my nether regions. I knew what it meant. That I had better take my medicine before the *turista* revisited me.

"Ernesto," I said, trying to conceal, for Jeet's sake, my distaste for the man, "could you please get my purse?"

"Your purse?"

"My handbag."

"The little black one, yes?"

"Yes."

He yanked a cord and then a maid appeared. He told her to get the purse. She disappeared and returned with it. "You are dismissed," he told the woman, and she nodded and went away.

I don't think I could handle having servants. I'm not mean enough. I would be thanking them, and next thing you know, they'd be ordering me around, I bet.

Anyway, I opened my purse and pulled out the

tiny liquor bottle containing the potion that the folks at the *farmacia* had prepared for me.

"Oh," Ernesto said, seeing that it was a liquor bottle. "You would like a drink." The words were harmless, but he said it in a sleazy way, as if I were making some sort of overt sexual overture.

You scum, I thought, and at the same time one of those idea lightbulbs, like in comic strips, went off for me.

"Oh, not at all," I cooed. "It's for you. A present. A special liqueur."

Ernesto seemed pleased. "I will get glasses for us," he said. He didn't ring for a servant this time. He rubbed his hands together and then went off himself. He returned with two tiny crystal glasses, green glass serpents coiling around their elegant fluted bowls.

Serpents. How appropriate.

But Ernesto had gotten the glasses himself. Ordinarily, I knew just from the little I'd observed, he'd have dispatched the maid. So he did think something was up here.

I know, you're going to accuse me of being superficial. You're going to say that I was fine when the cop who looked like Jimmy Smits was flirting with me, but that now, with this overweight old man, I'm grossed out.

Well, you're right. Except that there was something clean about Ramon Pedras, something that said that flirting was all it was, and it would stop right there.

Quinto, on the other hand, would have been on me in a minute if I'd given him anything resembling hope. I just knew that somehow, and don't ask me how. Women do know these things, we have to. Otherwise we'd be jumped in the streets and in elevators.

He held the glasses while I poured. I was surprised by how steady my hands were. I guess it's years of riding, years of being in hairy situations and pretending not to be afraid so the horse won't pick up on it. Or maybe just plain stubbornness, I don't know.

"Very tasty," he said, sipping. And in a way that I know he thought was very meaningful, he licked his lips.

I lifted my glass and glugged the contents.

"It is almond, no? Almond, with a hint of peach."

"Almond, yes," I said. "You are very astute. But then, you are a world-famous gourmet." And one who isn't going to have diarrhea anytime soon, I thought.

"Ah, yes, that is so," he said, holding the glass, the amber medicine coating the sides of its bowl, up to the light. Then he went into some rap about brandy, about how the quality of it could be measured by the length of time the residue clings to the glass. "So it is with the liqueur," he went on. The gourmet discourses about libations. Pretty soon he'd be pronouncing what he'd tasted "reckless" or "daring" or "amusing," and talking about sunlight on the various sides of the vineyard.

God, I knew the type. Jeet and I had made fun of that pompous sort of person often enough. Where was Jeet when I needed him?

"I'll have another bottle brought to you tomorrow," I said. "It's, uh, private stock."

"Private," he said. "How very charming."

Was it my imagination or had he moved closer? His breath seemed to wash right over me, hot and sticky. Pig breath, I thought.

And then I knew I was going to vomit.

I pushed him and the bedcovers back in a single motion, my hand clapped over my mouth. I headed for the door to the hall, but I heard Ernesto behind me shouting, "No! There! To the right!"

I turned abruptly and opened what I'd thought was a closet and the next thing I knew I was, as they say, kneeling before the porcelain god, puking my guts out.

Well, I consoled myself, when I was finally able to stand up and flush, at least that would have cooled Ernesto Quinto's ardor.

I was not wrong.

And then, blessedly, Jeet was back.

It seemed the manager of the hotel had given Jeet a hard time about moving our things, saying that he'd assured the policeman, Ramon Pedras, that Jeet would not. Jeet found him unbudgeable. Therefore, Jeet was sorry, but he was going to have to take me back to the hotel with him.

Ernesto, I think, would ordinarily have intervened, thrown his weight around, as it were. Since he'd stood outside the bathroom, though, and listened to me vomit, I think, really, he was glad to see me go.

I have never been able to contract those ailments

that emphasize one's fragility—you know, the sort where you sink deep into a nest of satin pillows, your hair prettily arrayed around you. This one time, though, I was awfully glad of it.

I remembered one other narrow escape from lechery, a boss of Jeet's who had somehow misinterpreted something I'd said. He'd nudged me and, like Ernesto, had winked. *"Toujours l'amour,"* he'd said, "Tonight for sure." God! What sort of woman would respond to an approach like that? Did these men go to the Clarence Thomas School of Sexual Conquest or what?

Jeet tried to cheer me on the bumpy ride back down the hill, saying that Ernesto was the cousin of a famous rider, a man who'd ridden jumpers for the Mexican equestrian team.

Like I cared.

I stared out the car window at the winking lights of San Miguel, smiling at the man with the burros who was making his way up the hill as we went down. The scene was probably exactly what you might have seen forty or fifty years earlier, except that the man was wearing running shoes instead of sandals.

It must still be early, I thought as we passed the Parroquia. It looked, in the moonlight, like a wedding cake adrip with thick, pink frosting. I felt better all of a sudden.

"We never did have dessert," I said to Jeet. "Let's stop someplace and get some."

"If you can handle bananas Foster," Jeet said, "I

know just the place. But are you sure you're up to it?"

I wasn't sure. Still, I said, "I'm always up to something gooey and flaming." No kidding, I would probably rise up from my deathbed for a good dessert.

"Try me," I went on. "If I can't eat it myself, I'll at least have the pleasure of watching you eat it." Because Jeet was always up for gooey and flaming himself. What's more, he ate with gusto, kind of X-rated eating. Like that scene in *Tom Jones*, or the one in *Flashdance*, all slurps and gluttonous smacks. "Please?" I said, the clincher.

Jeet tooled the Fiesta up one street and down another, watching the big arrows painted on buildings at each intersection. I don't know what the color-blind do in San Miguel, because a red arrow means you stop, and a black one gives you the right of way. All of the corners are blind, and so you just kind of trust as you skiddle about. It seems to work, though there's a lot of tire and brake squeals to be heard.

Jeet eventually pulled up in front of a place from which wild salsa music belled.

"Olé!" I said, bounding out of the car. I was still a little on the shaky side, but I thought if I acted perky, I'd eventually feel that way.

We had to walk across the dance floor in order to get to one of the tables. There were wall-to-wall couples dirty-dancing in that sexy, stooped-down salsa way. The male partner of one couple winked at me as I went by and said he was glad to see I hadn't been bothered by the murder earlier in the day.

It was Officer Ramon Pedras.

"I'm here for the bananas," I quipped. "What's your excuse?" I felt I could banter with him this way, I don't know exactly why. You know how you just fall into a way of behaving with someone, don't you?

"Señora," Pedras murmured just beneath the pulsing music. "Do you know how long it has been since we have had a murder in San Miguel?"

"No."

"Seven years," he said. "Seven years, and then *you* came to town, and just like that, there is one."

He was kidding, right? Right.

"We all have our talents," I said, but just to have a snappy reply. After I'd said it, of course, I realized that I could be wrong. About the kidding, I mean. And if I were, it would have been an incredibly stupid remark.

CHAPTER 7

That morning, Jeet and I presented ourselves at the local police station, which was conveniently located along one side of the Jardín.

We sat on a hard wooden bench.

"I wish we'd had some breakfast," Jeet said, eyeing a vendor just beyond the door who was carrying a tray of *chicherones*, hunks of fried pigskin. I could see that Jeet was wondering if my tummy could take sitting beside him while he scarfed one down.

"Don't," I said.

Then I felt a presence beside me, a young Mexican girl dressed as though she was about to take her first Holy Communion, all ribbons and white lace—a confection. "Bimbo, señora?" she asked.

I was stunned. "No, I'm a housewife, actually," I said, feeling Jeet rudely nudging my side.

"We'll take two," he said, digging in his pocket and handing her a bill.

"Gracias." She beamed, offering us the choice from her tray.

I stared down at the little cakes to learn that Bimbo was, in Mexico, the equivalent of, say, the com-

pany that makes the Hostess Twinkie. I picked out
two of the cello-wrapped cakes and she moved on.

We were ushered up a staircase and into a
large—nay, palatial—office overlooking a courtyard. I stood at the window and looked down at a
corps of police officers doing military sorts of ma-
neuvers; you know, right turn, left turn, that kind
of thing.

And they were *all* wearing screwdrivers in place
of guns. So it wasn't just a little idiosyncrasy of
Pedras.

"Jeet, come here, look," I said.

But just then Officer Pedras appeared.

He was a true detective, a man who intuited
things. "You are wondering, señora, why we do not
carry guns?"

"Yes," I said, amazed at his acuity.

His eyes twinkled, and the merest hint of a smile
appeared at the corners of his mouth. "It is because, until you came to our town, we handled only
traffic offenses. Because, until you came to our
town, traffic offenses were the only offenses. Now,
however—"

"Now see here," Jeet interrupted. He couldn't tell
Pedras was teasing. Which made me feel incredibly
proud of Jeet. I mean, here he was, terrified that
we would end up in a Mexican jail and yet actually
sticking his neck out by standing up for me.

And Pedras backed off, too. "You are quite right,"
he admitted. "I was making a bad joke. In truth,
the entire matter of the demise of the blacksmith
has been taken care of and you are both free to go."

Jeet's brows shot up, as did mine. Jeet turned to me and mouthed, "Ernesto."

"Wait a minute," I said. "What do screwdrivers have to do with handling traffic offenses?"

"Robin," Jeet tried, as in *Don't push your luck.*

"No, it's all right," Pedras assured. "Señora, when a person has accumulated a number of parking violations, we take from them their license plates, removing them with the screwdriver. You see?" He made turning gestures with his right hand in the air. "And then the person must pay to have the license plates back."

"Ah," I said.

"Ro-bin," Jeet repeated, doing the two-syllable thing I told you about, the one that means *Enough already.*

And so he and I made our way back down the stairs. Meanwhile, he tossed the Bimbo cakes into a trash bin.

"Hey," I said.

"We're free and clear," he said. "We can have a real breakfast now."

"Where?"

"I don't know. Let's walk until we come to a likely place."

And so we did, holding hands and ambling through the narrow cobblestoned streets.

The basic morning activity—of the hired help at least—seemed to be sweeping. What was there to sweep? Bougainvillea droppings. I kid you not. There were people out there with brooms sweeping fallen blossoms from the foot-wide sidewalks to the gutters of the street. This is trash in San Miguel de Allende!

And on the balconies and terraces, which everyone in San Miguel seemed to have, there was hosing down going on. Walking could be treacherous, what with little falls of water coming from drain spouts built into the walls for this purpose.

And there were dogs, dogs barking at us from the terraces up above. All of them seemed to have had the same sire, too, a kind of Benji-Basenji combination.

"Which could be what they're rinsing up there," Jeet warned.

We were more careful about getting water dumped on us from overhead then.

But even that seemed sweet, picturesque.

We walked through Benito Juarez Park, a mass of healthy-looking vegetation. On the tallest tree there, three white egrets duked it out for the uppermost branch. Their beaks locked, they jerked each other around until finally one of them had triumphed.

And just beyond the park, in a public fountain, the burro man, his huge sombrero shading his features, rinsed his hands. His burros grazed nearby on some weeds that had sprouted up between the cobblestones.

"Oh God, Jeet," I said, "I just love it here."

He squeezed my arm.

"What are you going to do today?" I asked him.

"I'm going to a cactus orchard," he said. Prickly-pear cactus is grown for food down here, and so it's planted on purpose and in rows so that the *tuna*, the meat of the cactus, can be harvested. "And you?"

"I guess I'll go back out to Milagro," I said.

You know the notion of the pathetic fallacy that we're taught in English class in school? It's a romantic concept, that nature will somehow mirror what is going on in life.

Well, it's hogwash. Because if it were true, the sun would have dimmed as I uttered those words, and it didn't, I assure you. It washed over the streets and the walls and the gardens just as bright as ever, as though nature agreed that going out to Milagro was a heads-up thing to do.

All I have to say is, thank God I took a bit of a precaution.

I went to La Conexión first, and put in a call to Lola back in the United States.

I mean, I had to find out about Sturmgeist, right? If that guy I had seen heading back to Marilee's was in fact Sturmgeist's groom. Because—this was something I hadn't said to Jeet or to Officer Pedras—it was entirely possible that poor Felipe had been murdered for telling me how to get to the farm in the first place.

Think about it.

So I ditched Jeet with a promise to meet him for *comida corrida*, which is a kind of late lunch, and then there I was, in what is sort of a combination phone-call, fax, and camera store, trying to get through. And the upshot was that it cost me two pesos a minute to hear about seven simultaneous conversations in what seemed like four separate

languages (one of which was pig Latin) while Lola
shouted in the background, "Hello? hello? hello?"
then "Robin? Robin? Is this you?" and meanwhile I
shouted about Marilee and then about Sturmgeist
and the photocopy I'd made three years ago at
Texas A&M and how I needed it to be faxed to La
Conexión posthaste. I even remembered where the
photocopy was—Scotch-taped on the wall over my
riding helmets.

Everyone in the place was staring at me when I
finished and I still had no way of knowing whether Lola had heard me or not. "If a fax comes in," I
told the counterman, "please let me know." Then
I told him where Jeet and I were staying. And just
to be on the safe side, I told him that if we weren't
at the hotel, we might be at Casa Quinto, Ernesto's place.

God, Mexico is wonderful. Here and in restaurants and wherever you are, the people try to
accommodate you. It's not like America, where
they scream at you, "You can't sit there," or "We
don't make it that way," or "We can't do that." No.
They try to accommodate you. In Mexico, the cus-
tomer is still always right.

"Very good, señora," the counterman said, smiling.

So I drove back out to where I'd last seen
Marilee. I passed the drive that led into the golden
hill, because it was a cinch that the Jaguar roadster hadn't—couldn't get up it.

And besides, it led to the stable, which made
sense, since Felipe was the blacksmith.

There had to be another drive farther on, a drive

that could be negotiated. A drive that led to the house.

The question was, should I use it, or should I reconnoiter on foot?

Then my body solved the problem for me.

I parked at the bottom of the next drive and ran for the bushes, full tilt.

I cursed myself for forgetting to take my *turista* medicine that morning. Soon, however, I was cursing myself for more. I was cursing myself for forgetting my purse, which had the facial tissues in it.

And meanwhile I made do with—well, fortunately—very large, very broad, very soft, and very plentiful leaves.

Well, maybe my animal senses were keener because I'd been reduced to a sort of animal state, I don't know. The thing is, I could hear the sound of horses. Horses grazing, kind of snorting the way they do as they walk around.

So as soon as I was able, I had my trousers back where they belonged and I was pushing my way through the foliage toward the sound.

And lo!

I came to the top of a rise and saw a series of fields all bordered with stone walls that were—well, this doesn't sound very nice, but it was actually quite lovely—stump-topped. The stumps themselves were gnarled, with arms jutting out from them, like driftwood. Come to think of it, maybe they were roots rather than stumps, but in any case, there would be maybe a two-foot wall of stone with these stumps atop it, maybe adding another foot and a

half. It was very picturesque, the kind of thing you
see in *National Geographic.*

Because there were so many pastures, so many
divisions, the walls looked beautiful in a wild and
primitive kind of way. I don't know how the stumps
were fixed there, but they had to be immovable, because horses would very quickly discover that they
could be tumbled if in fact they could.

Horses are like that.

They aren't as bad as cows, but still, if they're in
one field, they always want to be in the field that's
adjacent. It's just a fact.

So these stumps were somehow installed there
for good.

But I don't know why I was so intent on the
stumps, because the horses were the thing that
must have caused the locals to name the place
Milagro—miracle.

It seemed a miracle indeed.

For as far as the eye could see, there were big
bay horses, maybe fifty of them, and they were
identical. Wide white blazes, white socks.

Identical right down to the white handprint
birthmark on each and every belly. And yes, it was
the same birthmark that the horse Marilee had
shown me years ago had had.

And I got it, the Sturmgeist birthmark. It had to
be. Sturmgeist himself was probably here.

I guess I should have gone back to the car then
and there and located Officer Pedras, although I
didn't. For one thing, I didn't know what the ille-
gality of breeding look-alike horses might be. I

mean, even if it were something super high-tech, like cloning, what sort of offense was that?

And also, I admit it, I wanted to see the house that was attached to all of this, the place that Marilee Hart was allegedly in charge of.

So I kept walking until I heard the sound of car doors slamming. Car doors slamming, followed by the sound of engines revving up.

My God.

They would see my car down at the end of the driveway. They would see the Fiesta, take the license-plate number down, and find out, with a little bribe—*mordida*, they say here—that it was rented out to Jeet and me.

Well, to Jeet. He was the one who had his name on all our credit cards.

I might as well keep going now and check out the house as I'd planned. I mean, what was there to lose? But I crept up close enough to the drive to be able to see the cars as they passed me—which of course they'd have to do.

I did make sure I was out of sight myself, though.

My heart lurched. There was a flatbed truck, and on it, the sorry red pickup truck that had been Felipe's.

Then there was that Jaguar, with its low, curved, sexy lines.

Then something even fancier, a limo, black, a Bentley, maybe. The windows were tinted, but they'd been rolled a good part of the way down so that I could see who was being driven inside.

It was Ernesto Quinto.

Somehow, I was not surprised.

* * *

Of course, seeing the house was out of the question now. The fact that these men had that truck meant they were implicated in Felipe's murder. And while cloning may be no big deal, murder, in every country I knew about, still was. I needed to get out of there, and I needed to reach Ramon Pedras.

I went back through the bushes, and sure enough, the Jag was parked beside my Fiesta, and the groom guy—except that if he was a Jaguar owner, he was probably more than a groom, so let's just call him Marilee's boyfriend—was going through it. He was exceedingly tall. That was about right, if I remembered him beside the big German stud horse in the photo I'd Xeroxed. Yeah.

One thing, he didn't have to bribe anyone about tracing the license plates because he had my Sportsac open and he was sliding my wallet back into it.

Would he connect me with the blacksmith, Felipe? Felipe had, after all, my name on a piece of paper, but whoever had stabbed him may not have realized it. I mean, the paper was still in Felipe's hand.

Fingerprints, I thought. Interpol. I could find out who this groom guy was. I could take down *his* license number.

When he roared off, I got into the Fiesta and wrote the number down and then drove back to town, but Officer Ramon Pedras was not to be found. My Spanish wasn't sufficient to explain what was on my mind, and anyway, I was nearly

late for meeting Jeet. So I didn't wait, but instead
searched out Posada Carmina, our planned rendez-
vous for *comida corrida*.

There was Jeet, a bright array of mango and
melon and papaya in front of him, and a bevy of admirers surrounding his table. I guessed that the
publicity stuff he'd been doing—the newspaper ar-
ticle on him and the TV coverage—had appeared.

But I worried about the anonymity he was so
careful to preserve back home. It's true that this
was Mexico, but jeez . . . Jeet had already been told
in no uncertain terms by his editor that when his
book, the food memoir, came out, he could *not* have
his picture on it. Because Jeet and I go around to
Austin restaurants on the q.t. and evaluate them.
If the restaurant folk knew Jeet on sight, they'd
treat him differently, you see?

Well, anyway, my husband sure wasn't worried
about his anonymity now. I'm not a hundred percent sure, but I think I actually saw him signing
his autograph on one of the menus.

I approached the table and Jeet introduced me as
his wife. Then he said, "If you'll excuse us . . . ?"
and the mob, ever so ruly, faded off.

"Good day?" Jeet asked.

I was about to tell him all about it when—yes. I
stood up, wild-eyed, and the waiters, recognizing
the look on my face as one of the key symptoms,
pointed in the direction of the john.

I guess I was there for quite a while. Because
when I emerged, all of the wrought-iron tables

were empty and, in fact, the waiters were playing dominoes at one of them.

I staggered through my makeshift Spanish with a waiter, who, as far as I could tell, was trying to say that Jeet had been kidnapped.

"Kidnapped?" I said, thumbing through my phrase book. The best I could do for verification was *niño*, which means "child," and *dormir*, which means, "to sleep." It wasn't working. *"Cabrito?"* I tried. That's a goat. You could get "kid" from that, maybe.

"Ah, sí!" The waiter brightened.

At first I thought he was jubilant about verifying that my husband had indeed been kidnapped. But almost instantly I realized that most probably the waiter thought I was asking if the restaurant *served* cabrito. Which, this being Mexico, they of course did.

So I was stymied, helplessly mired in translation problems. I would have to—and you know by now this is not one of my strengths—reason it out.

Well, okay, here goes.

No one was going to kidnap Jeet, an American tourist, from a popular San Miguel de Allende restaurant in broad daylight.

I could therefore leave the restaurant with confidence and go back to our hotel. And Jeet would be there.

But see, here's why I have such a problem with reasoning things out. What I'd said makes sense, right? But then what about the little voice inside that was asking why Jeet had left the restaurant to begin with? Why he didn't at least leave a note?

Do reasoning people not have such a voice? Or do they just ignore it?

Anyway, I thought of how I'd seen Jeet when I'd entered the restaurant. He'd been surrounded by admirers, beaming at the array of fresh fruit on his plate.

Ha!

Maybe he was wrong about peeled fruit being okay to eat. Maybe *he* had *turista* now, too. I pictured him running through the streets, trying to make it to our hotel. Because I, after all, had been occupying the restaurant's only john.

Yeah, that was bound to be it.

So I hustled a bit, sure I'd find Jeet—and another little bottle of my trusty *turista* medicine—waiting for me.

Or waiting for us. Because I'd share the medicine with him, of course, and then I'd tell him and we'd laugh together about my having given Ernesto Quinto some and pretending it was a liqueur.

Oh-oh. That twinge again.

I began to hustle more earnestly, aware that I'd better not get caught out on the street between bathrooms.

At that point, the worst possible situation I could envision was to find my husband occupying ours when I needed it.

Had I but known.

CHAPTER 8

When I got to the hotel the desk clerk was in a tizzy. They had a fax for me. It had been hand-carried over by someone at La Conexión.

This evidently made the desk clerk think I was a very big deal.

I thanked him and tipped him, and tore into it right there. It was a two-page communication from Lola, scrawled on LoCo Farms stationery. And it read:

> *Article in* Das Pferd *says Sturmgeist bought and kept in seclusion in Argentina by old guy who claimed the horse should not be bred because of a defect. Did not say what defect was. Sturmgeist should be twenty-one years old now and still in Argentina but has never been bred. Your old Xerox pic follows.*

Defect. Like a handprint, maybe. A handprint you tried to hide with shoe polish.

I turned to the fax-quality copy of my already poor photocopy of the horse. With, yes, no mistaking it, even given the way the picture had reproduced, the Jaguar guy beside him.

Bingo.

So they'd stolen Sturmgeist and bred him like crazy. Which was why Marilee had pulled a gun. Except those horses in the fields were two or three years old. If they'd stolen the stallion that long ago, wouldn't Lola have found some reference to it?

Except that a stolen Sturmgeist might mean that maybe Jeet *had* been kidnapped after all! I mean, they'd have seen the Fiesta near Milagro and they might have thought the person spying on them had been Jeet.

They'd found my purse, but maybe they thought I'd accompanied Jeet. In any case, Jeet, to them, must have seemed like the threat.

You're jumping to conclusions again, I warned myself, trying to imagine Jeet right upstairs in our hotel room even as I vaulted up the staircase toward it.

The only absolutely clear thing, I told myself, was that something shady *was* going on. Because Sturmgeist *had* been bred once to produce Gentian and maybe now was being bred right here in San Miguel de Allende, or just outside of it.

But surely that wasn't reason enough to kidnap an American citizen.

I called Jeet's name as I jammed the key into the lock and turned. He'll be there, he'll be there, I told myself, hollering, "Jeet, Jeet?" even when I'd opened the door and encountered the strange stillness that meant he wasn't.

I walked in, though the room was a mess—drawers open, stuff everywhere.

It's been tossed, I thought, borrowing the jargon of the American detective novel in an attempt to be flip. It didn't toughen me, though. Instead, I had a hollowness inside that was mostly fear.

Better fear, I consoled myself, than a galloping sense of panic.

Think, I tried. Think.

How much danger could Jeet be in? Would anybody kill him? I kept thinking somehow that being an American would count for a lot, but I could be wrong.

And beyond that, could I convince anyone in authority that Jeet was in any danger at all? Maybe I could pull that waiter from the restaurant in to corroborate my story, but he'd been so, I don't know, sanguine about telling me. He wasn't aware of any peril.

And who else was under threat? Maybe not just Jeet. Maybe Marilee was in danger, too.

I mean, hadn't these guys killed Felipe? Didn't they have to be the ones?

And Ernesto Quinto was up to his eyebrows in it, also.

Calm down, I instructed myself. Chill.

Then I tried to think of objections Pedras or whoever might make. Think.

"Why Jeet?" they would say.

Because the bad guys *had* traced the Fiesta to him after all.

But wasn't it me they'd want? My name was also on the car thing.

That was a tougher one to answer.

Mexico is still into the macho thing, I tried. And so it had been impossible for them to imagine a woman acting on her own.

I kept going with this line of thought. And, I went on, because they probably thought that as my husband, Jeet was privy to and maybe even responsible for everything that I'd been up to.

Yeah, that would do it. Even Ramon Pedras would buy that.

Okay. I snatched up a fanny pack and put another little bottle of *turista* medicine inside. I mean, I didn't want to be in the middle of a big explanation to the police if and when the urge struck again.

And maybe before I'd go to the police, I reasoned, it wouldn't hurt to have somebody stateside who knew what was going on. In case the police didn't believe me or, worse, somehow ended up by putting *me* in jail.

I mean, anything can happen in a foreign country, right?

So I fought the instinct to run to Pedras's office and instead moved off to La Conexión again, where for two pesos a minute I bellowed everything I knew into the phone and hoped that Lola—or in this case, her answering machine—could hear me over the static. Of course, by filling Lola in at the decibel level I was forced to use, I also filled in everyone working and loitering at La Conexión, plus any person within, say, a half-block radius of the building.

Still, it could not be helped.

Then I ran along the cobblestones to the police station, stopping at the entrance to catch my breath and attempt an air of insouciance that would make Ramon Pedras believe.

I explained the whole thing to him—slowly and calmly, too—but all the while I was talking, I could tell he wasn't buying it. He was shaking his head, no, no, no, and he shook it especially violently when I tried to convince him that Ernesto Quinto was a part of the entire thing.

"Señora," he said, "let us go, sit quietly, have a *postre* and a cup of cafe—"

"Officer Pedras," I said, "this is serious. This is a matter of life and death." I'd been wrong to tease along with him the way I had earlier. It had convinced him I was a bubblehead or something. He seemed, in fact, eager to spend time with me, but not the way I meant.

"Señora. Let us talk calmly about this. But away from this place."

Hadn't I *been* calm? Maybe not by Mexican police standards. "Oh, all right," I said. Maybe the police station had been infiltrated by wrongdoers. That was another possible reason for Pedras wanting to spirit me away.

So I followed him to a place called El Otro Café. Even though it was in the very heart of town, we found the burros and their owner parked outside. The animals were carrying huge milk cans this time, although previously their burdens had been bags of something.

In an attempt to be light, I conveyed this information to Pedras. My plan was to sound like a reasonable person, not someone in the throes of need.

"Oh, yes," he said. "They bring everything down from the mountains, even soil for the plants we grow here."

"Topsoil," I offered.

"Sí."

"They must bring an awful lot of it in," I suggested, "since there are so many plants."

"Sí. Here in San Miguel, we owe the burros much."

I wanted to change the subject back to Jeet and what was going on, but I didn't want to do it too soon. I had to convince Pedras that what I was alleging was a real possibility, which meant leading up to it with chitchat.

Sort of the way Len Reasoner, my vet, always advised that things be done.

But I was fresh out of chitchat for the nonce. I sat in stymied silence, which forced Pedras to speak.

"I burned two burros last winter," he said. "And most of my friends, they burned at least one."

"Huh?" I said, tuning in.

"I burned two—"

He stopped when he saw how I was staring at him. I was overreacting, I suppose. But to think that I was about to place my trust in a man who would burn these animals for heat in a city where the weather rarely dipped below forty, was too much to bear.

"What is wrong, señora?" he paused and asked.

What was wrong right then was everything. Bur-

ros on a spit, pigs with cherries in their eye sockets. Husbands missing.

I stood. "I can't stay here," I said. "I can't even sit
at the same table with you, señor. I don't want . . ."
And then, surprising even me, tears spilled down
my cheeks.

He reached across the table and took my hand. "I
regret anything I may have said to offend you," he
said, tugging at my hand to encourage me back
into the chair. "Please." He was glancing anxiously
around, too, which made me think that he was worried about what others might think.

What else could I do? I had no other place to
turn. I was stricken with exhaustion and sank into
the seat like a stone. I tried to explain what he'd
said that had sent me over the edge.

"I know you think Americans are sentimental.
About animals." I sniffed. "And maybe I did grow
up watching Walt Disney, I don't know. But the
point is, if you can cook pigs and burn burros, you
probably don't care very much about Jeet either,
and talking to you will just be a great big waste of
time." I had said all this in big sucking gulps, you
know how you do, kind of trying to talk without
crying again.

And just when I was thinking how pathetic he
must have found me, he burst out laughing.

He'd let go of my hand when I'd sat again, but
now he reached out and grabbed my wrist, knowing, I suppose, that I was preparing to run out of
the restaurant and away from him. Somewhere
way back in my mind I remembered having heard

that in Spanish there's no word to designate a pet. I shouted this at him. And I cried even harder.

He offered me a cotton hanky and I took it, blew my nose.

I could feel the eyes of the other people in the café upon me.

"Oh, you Americans!" Pedras said jovially. "It is just an expression, burning burros. The burros, they bring firewood from the mountains, so that when we say we burned two burros, what we mean is, it is two burro *loads* we have burned. The burros—"

"The burros!" I interrupted him, my tears and the attendant pathos swept aside. "The burros!" I said.

Now the other patrons decided I was truly loony. They all waited, no one daring to look away.

I pulled my chair closer to the table and leaned across it. Then I lowered my voice. "The man with the burros was there at the overlook when Felipe, the blacksmith, told me about Milagro. And I saw the burro man one other time, too. I can't remember when." Was it when we were driving off from Ernesto Quinto's? I couldn't recall. The point was, the man with the burros—the man in the sombrero wearing running shoes—seemed to be everywhere.

My voicing this seemed to make Ramon Pedras think I'd ventured farther around the bend than before. In fact, his tone, the deadpan way he formed the words, indicated this. "You think the man with the burros is a part of this massive scheme," he said, as if, thanks to my having made this statement, I'd clinched things. A sanity hearing would not be required. They could simply commit me, carry me away, have me making clay ashtrays and raffia coasters and thick cotton potholders for the rest of my days.

"Don't close your mind, Ramon," I said, and then I hiccuped.

In response, he rolled his eyes, a mere step away from saying, "Ro-bin . . ."

But I was wrong. He made his voice all deep and throaty. "Robin," he said, smiling at me.

Oh God.

"Señor Pedras," I retreated.

"Robin," he said again, leaning closer.

"I'm a happily married woman." I hiccuped. "At least I was when I had a husband. What I'm trying to point out is that my husband is missing and that spooky things are going on just a hop, skip, and"—I paused to hic—"a jump away from here."

He seemed to get part of the point. "Señora, your husband is probably fine, and your friend, this Marilee, she is probably just as fine. You will go back to Texas and have babies and forget about all of this."

I didn't care how sexist and condescending that was. I did care that he take Jeet's disappearance seriously. And Felipe's murder, too.

"I want the *federales*," I said. "The man with the burros is right outside this café, and you refuse to even question him. . . ."

He leaned across the table and whispered, "No, señora, you do not want the *federales*. But if it will make you any happier, I will question this man and possibly his burros as well." He rolled his eyes, tossed a bill on the table, and led the way to the street.

Where we discovered that the man with the burros was long gone.

"He was eavesdropping to see how much we knew," I insisted.

"Or else he was making a delivery," Pedras said.

Why had I thought of this man as a potential savior?

The expression on my face must have said as much, because he said, "If I may point out, the burro man did not follow us to the café. He was here when we arrived."

I hated to admit that he was right, so I didn't. Instead I fished through my purse for the slip of paper on which I'd written the Jaguar's license number.

"Here's one more thing," I said, handing it to him. "I need to know whose license plate—"

He peered at it and interrupted me. "Wolf Heimlich," he said.

"What?"

"The license number. It is for a Jaguar roadster owned by Wolfgang Heimlich."

"Impossible. You can't possibly know that without looking it up."

He pulled his screwdriver from its little holster and waved it about. "Ah, but I can, señora, if I have taken the plate and returned it to its owner often enough."

Marilee had taken up with a scofflaw.

"But will you help me?" I asked.

"I *am* helping," he said, with an elaborate shrug. He lifted his hands in supplication. "How much more help can one man be?"

One thing was rapidly becoming clear to me: I was on my own. If Jeet and if Marilee were to be saved, I, Robin Vaughan, was the one who had to do it. I hiccuped again and stalked off.

First thing I did after leaving Officer Pedras was go to Ernesto's. I walked this time, huffing up the narrow, winding streets that led to the edge of town.

My map was wearing at the folds, so I didn't dare consult it much. Instead I tried to memorize the streets I needed to watch for.

I wound around, ever higher, out of the old part of San Miguel into a downright shabby section that had seemed so small when we'd driven through it.

Now I saw that it was more than a city block long, a section where bone-thin dogs regarded me warily, where doors opened on bleak hallways and meaty smells wafted heavily into the street.

I saw sewage, too, in an open canal.

Words like *cholera* and *typhoid* occurred to me.

And then I was, literally, above all this, in an open section of newly cobbled road far above old San Miguel.

The newer homes—architectural delicacies that skirted the big green canyon's edge—loomed ahead.

Ernesto's, of course, was one, and from this vantage point, I could see that it was double the size of its neighbors.

I couldn't help but think of the enclave of the

poor squeezed into a narrow ribbon of space between this new bold stand of opulence above and the more sedate splendor of the old city below.

It must pain the poor people daily, I thought, to see all this wealth on display.

I felt the eyes of the poor people upon me and wondered if behind their friendly greetings—because they all did smile and bid me hello—they thought of me as an oppressor, a rich American señora on her way back home. Someone who would complain that the floor tile hadn't been waxed enough, or a shirt collar not pressed to her satisfaction.

God, was I becoming political?

At last I reached the aeries that were the bigger homes. Ernesto's, thank God, was the first.

I'll say this about Mexican architecture: privacy is exceedingly well maintained. There are all those walls around the houses, for one thing, to keep peering onlookers away. Ernesto's wall was doubly secure. It had bits of broken bottle glass embedded in the surface all along the top. Primitive as it seemed, it was very effective.

I'm saying that Ernesto Quinto's place, street-side, was impregnable.

Of course, there was that canyon on the other side. On that end, the house was completely open. But I'd have to dress in cruddy clothes to go down into the canyon that it perched on and come up the other side in order to see. It was probably at least a mile, say half a mile, down and another half a mile back up. A mile of cactus and scrub and maybe rattlesnakes and tarantulas.

Nah.

Also, because the other side was pretty far away, I'd need binoculars of my own or a telescope like Ernesto's or something in order to really be able to spy on things.

So coming here hadn't been a great idea after all.

I sat on the steps that led to Ernesto's massive double front door. My legs, which are pretty strong, actually ached from the steep climb. I was breathing pretty hard, too, though it could have been the thinness of the mountain air.

What now? I wondered. What now?

Milagro was the only alternative. And for that I'd need the car. I cursed myself for having walked all the way to Ernesto's and couldn't even remember now why I had.

Oh—it was because I'd thought I'd be less visible than the Fiesta. If I needed to be, that is. So I'd have to remember that when I drove to Milagro, and park the car behind some brush.

You're doing this for Jeet, I reminded myself.

I got out of the Fiesta once I'd found a cactus stand sufficient to park behind and looked around.

I, too, needed cover, I decided. I attempted to disguise myself, breaking off several branches so that I could, if I needed to, make like a shrub. I silently thanked William Shakespeare for that one because, if you'll remember, that's how Burnham Wood came to Dunsinane.

Jeet isn't the only one with esoteric literary knowledge.

Jeet. Just the mental mention of his name gave me a pang. Maybe all of this *was* something I'd trumped up in my head. I mean, that hotel room. Hadn't Jeet often left our bedroom in the same disheveled state? Or the kitchen, when he was looking, say, for his nutmeg grater or the garlic press that had been in his family umpteen jillion years.

Jeet. Jeet and all the little things that made him who he is. No, I had to find him.

Except that after about a half mile of carrying the camouflaging branches over one stump-topped wall after another, my arms were ready to give out and I had to lay the branches down.

Jeet. I kept repeating his name like a mantra.

I passed through several fields of horses, and then through an enormous pasture where perhaps a hundred head of cattle milled about. The cows moved away as I approached, and I slipped through a gate into what was clearly the lawn.

Almost there. I came over a little rise and there it was, the house, a big stucco-and-beam thing that made Quinto's place and Hans Bell's, too, look like veritable dumps. Well, maybe not dumps, but it was their equal and more.

But I couldn't take time to rhapsodize about the architecture. I mean, after all, Jeet was probably being held somewhere inside. I could see him surrounded by men who were trying to force him to tell them what he knew about the horse.

And of course he didn't know squat.

I mean, he had probably tuned out while I was

going on and on about Sturmgeist, so that he wouldn't even recognize the horse's name.

Poor Jeet.

I didn't think they would kill him, though. It was one thing to kill Felipe, a Mexican national, but quite another to kill off Jeet. Especially since the publicity he'd garnered locally made him a kind of celebrity.

I advanced upon the house.

It was totally open, I mean, whole rooms that led to the out-of-doors, floor-to-ceiling expanses of glass that had been opened wide.

And there were all kinds of flowers; bougainvillea, and trumpet vine, and canna. There were birds chirping and little sculptured trees in pots.

If you were going to be held prisoner, you could do a lot worse.

I slipped into one of the rooms and looked about.

It was a kitchen. A kitchen as large as maybe our whole house back home on Primrose Farm. It was all rustic beams and Saltillo tile, with small decorative hand-hewn and hand-painted tile on the walls.

The paintings were of lizards and turtles, utterly charming.

There were primitive baskets laid out on a long enamel table, each bearing some dried herb or fresh vegetable. There were even odd veggies, like tomatillo.

There were little mortars and pestles, too, various sizes of them, as if someone were seriously into grinding spices. Myriad peppers—fresh green ones and gnarled brownish dry ones—were everywhere, too.

I knew if Jeet had been brought in here, even if it were at gunpoint, he would still be asking questions about the herbs and the peppers and equipment.

Just then an imperious-looking Mexican woman appeared. She was elegantly dressed in an ivory-colored linen sheath and extremely high heels. "Yes?" she asked.

"I'm the wife of Jeet Vaughan," I announced. I did it with a real edge in my voice. Attitude can carry you a long way.

"Oh, yes." She brightened. "I have heard much of Señor Vaughan."

"Is he here?" I tried.

She lost her cool, looked frightened. "He is coming here? Oh, no! I am not ready for anything of this magnitude!" She took the side of her hand and began wiping imaginary crumbs off an utterly spotless countertop. *"Ay, caramba!"* she said.

"No, wait," I told her. "I'm looking for Jeet Vaughan. Is he here? Because if he isn't here already, he isn't coming."

She sighed deeply. "Oh, no, señora, no. I could not imagine that he would come here, to me, to my humble *cocina.*"

"This is *your* house," I said, thinking, Ha! Marilee is a liar and a stable girl after all.

"Oh, no, I am housekeeper," she said. "It belongs to Señor Wolf and Señorita Marilee."

Señorita Marilee. So he was her boyfriend after all.

"And where is Señorita Marilee?" I asked.

"She is at the stable. In fact, she is the only one

here. Everyone has been given the day off because it is a feast day. Even I am to be off, but I returned, fearing I'd left something on the stove."

So Jeet *could* be here, I thought. That would explain their liberal leave policy.

Then the housekeeper looked out the window and gasped.

"What?" I said.

"The cows are out again," she said. "This is the third time this week."

Big deal.

"There will be the devil to pay," she continued.

I guessed she was talking about Wolf. "It wasn't you," I assured her. "I was the last one through the gate."

She looked wary.

I knew I had an edge and moved right along. "No one needs to know you were here," I told her. Or for that matter, I thought, that I am either.

"Well," she said, her voice losing all of its breathy urgency and returning to its original timbre. "O-kay. I will be going now. *Bueno*-bye."

"See you," I offered. It was clear that she was glad to be able to get out of there before Marilee saw those cows and accused her of turning them loose. Because you know how cows are, don't you? Cows get into everything, even worse than horses do. If it moves, cows will push it and then push it again. Cows are the reason barbed wire was invented, because they'll knock anything down.

And of course there wasn't any barbed wire here.

* * *

I made my way through the herd and found the stable, which was even more impressive from the front. You'll remember that I'd only seen the rear of it before. I don't know what it is about stucco and wrought iron, but it seems uncommonly lovely to me. Maybe because I think of it as fancy, and a stable, after all, rarely is.

Marilee was inside with that beautiful bay horse Gentian. The one I'd tried by accident to longe at the show. The horse, in fact, who started the whole thing.

At least, it appeared to be Gentian, though of course every horse I'd seen here looked exactly like him. She'd just finished tacking the horse up and was probably about to ride.

Marilee turned and saw me. "Robin," she said, shaking her head. "I can't believe you're back. You are such a colossal dope."

"I know that Jeet is here," I told her. "Where do you have him?"

"Jeet? You mean your husband?" She started to laugh. "Why would we have Jeet?"

I have to admit, it didn't seem as though she was pretending. But it couldn't be that he was there and she didn't know.

Still, I thought I'd try to get her to spill the beans about the parts she did know. "It isn't any use, Marilee. You'd better come clean."

Marilee paused, then put the reins up over the horse's head. She picked the halter up and put it on atop his bridle. Then she refastened the ties.

She did all of this very calmly, and I thought my ploy had failed.

My heart sank. It had sure worked three years ago, hadn't it? When she thought I knew more than I did and had confessed all?

"You'd better," I emphasized.

I watched her face. She had a little knit in her brow that, had it been my face, would have meant I was trying not to cry. And that first time back at her trailer, that was exactly what had happened, she'd begun to cry.

I glanced at her hands. She was clenching and unclenching them.

"You'd really better," I said again.

And she just sank, collapsed in on herself. "I knew it couldn't last," she said, crouching, her shoulders shaking. "I knew it. Because it's stealing. That's what it is. Oh, I knew we wouldn't get away with it. Even here."

I tried to bluff it out until I learned what *it* was. "That's right," I said. "It's stealing, all right." I had this enormous urge to wrap my arms around her, there-there fashion. I didn't yield to it, though.

"Except what does it hurt?" she asked me, looking at me now. She'd switched to belligerence, but the tears were coming still. "I mean, when you think about it, we're bringing wonderful, wonderful horses into the world, horses that otherwise wouldn't have been born."

"Sturmgeist babies!" I said, pulling a wadded-up napkin out of my pocket and handing it to her.

She nodded, wiped her eyes, blew her nose. "Sturmgeist," she said. "He's so prepotent," she went on. "I mean, they all look and move exactly like him."

Really prepotent stallions do come along. I had seen an auction at the King Ranch once, and every single one of the babies looked the way these babies did, exactly like their sire.

"So where is he?" I asked.

She looked at me and stopped crying. Even kind of laughed. "He's in Argentina. He's always been in Argentina. God," she said, "I've done it again. Let you trick me."

I guess I looked confused. She shook her head. "Artificial insemination, dummy."

I saw Len Reasoner in my mind's eye, approaching a mare in stocks.

"Wolf is the mastermind," I said, though I'd learned his name just a little while earlier. Still, he was the Jaguar guy, Sturmgeist's groom, so it had to be. Plus I wanted to sound as though I knew something.

She nodded. "He took the horse's semen. He did it for me that first time, and then we thought . . . well, why not? Why not do something on a bigger scale."

"Something that would make you rich."

"Yes."

There was a silence. We looked at each other across it.

"I didn't know it would end up like this," she said, and I saw her sorrow.

I moved toward her. She all but fell into my arms and started wailing again.

"It's all right, Marilee," I said. "Whatever it is."

"It started so innocently," she said. "Honest to God, it did."

I patted her.

She pulled back. "Do you believe me?" she asked me.

"I guess," I said.

"No, you have to," she shouted. "Because at first it was just me. Wolf saw me ride and he said, 'You need a really good horse if you're going to get any-place.'" She laughed a bit. "You know how that is, Robin," she said, thinking of Plum, I guess.

"Yeah," I said, "I know."

"Anyway, that's when he told me about Sturm-geist. About how this man he worked for down in Argentina wouldn't let Sturmgeist be bred. And that's how it happened, the first time. Wolf did it for me."

"But that would mean you'd known him—what?—years and years down the road." I couldn't remember how old Gentian had been, but five at least at the time of the Groundhog Classic.

"I don't mean we bred him right then," she said. "There was a Sturmgeist colt. A sort of test baby that Wolf wasn't going to tell anybody about. Be-cause he was kind of hoping, I think, that the handprint—the birthmark—wouldn't show up and he could talk his boss into breeding Sturmgeist af-ter all."

"But it did."

"Well, yeah, it did," she said. "Remember? You saw it."

I had seen it, right. "But so what?" I said. "How can a birthmark be such a big deal?"

"That was what Wolf couldn't understand. Why

this guy had bought the horse just so he wouldn't
be bred. He was an old Nazi or something."

I felt a shiver. I mean, a Nazi, wouldn't that explain it? No imperfect specimens or something? But
were she and Wolf crazy? I could just imagine this
Nazi guy waltzing in on them, saying, "Ve haf vays
of making you pay."

I said, "What if the owner of Sturmgeist finds
out?"

"He was ancient," Marilee scoffed. "He'd never
. . . but anyway, now he's dead."

"But back when he was alive . . ." I guided her,
wanting to hear it all. How she'd gone from person-
ally owning a Sturmgeist baby to creating a veritable Sturmgeist baby factory.

"Someone with money found out the way you
did," she said. "About Gentian. Someone offered to
back Wolf down here."

"Why here? Why Mexico?"

Marilee just rolled her eyes.

"You could get away with more," I offered.

"Well, sure. There's dressage down here, but really, not too many people are into it. The chances of
anyone saying, 'That's a Sturmgeist baby,' were
minimal. And we never show them. We just raise
them and break them and . . ." She started crying
again.

I waited, and eventually she was able to talk. I
wondered why she'd been overcome with emotion
again, but soon found out. "They decided to kill
Sturmgeist," Marilee sobbed. "And . . ." But she really lost it then.

"Kill Sturmgeist? That doesn't make any sense."

"But it does. Because the owner, the old Nazi, died and his son inherited everything. And he—the son—was going to stand Sturmgeist legally, and then all of our babies would be worth less money or something. I don't know."

I'd never been introduced to the mysteries of economics, and I reasoned that Marilee hadn't either, but in the rudimentary way that I was able to understand all of this, it seemed reasonable.

"Wolf loves Sturmgeist. In the beginning the whole thing was that he couldn't bear to have a horse of his quality go to his grave without siring babies. He freaked when they talked about killing the horse. He freaked, and now they know and . . ."

"Know what?" I prodded.

But suddenly her expression changed. Her hand went up to cover her mouth. "You're going to tell, aren't you?" She looked horrified.

"Yes," I said. "I have to. It *is* stealing."

"But there's nothing wrong with horses having a birthmark," she protested.

"Marilee, I agree. But that isn't the point." I didn't raise the issue of murder—Felipe's—right then. "The point is that Sturmgeist isn't yours."

"Well, yeah, but I can't have you do that, Robin," she said, still sniveling, but reaching down in a purposeful way into her grooming box. "I can't have you spoiling things for Wolf and me. Especially not now, when that Wolf's done something really—"

"Really what?" I jumped in. "You mean kidnapping Jeet, don't you?"

"Believe me. We do not have Jeet. What Wolf has done is brave and wonderful, but it isn't going to sit well with the people here." She paused and stared at the grooming box. Whatever she'd been feeling around for hadn't come into her hand. She squatted now and began a more concerted search.

"You mean it? You don't have Jeet."

"I mean it," she said, finally finding what she was looking for.

A pistol.

It was aimed right at me. It was small and black and deadly looking and it scared me in a way the shotgun hadn't. For one thing, she'd produced it specifically for me. It hadn't been, "Hey, what's that noise?" the way the shotgun had been brought out.

Gentian nickered, as though the pistol were a treat instead of the threat it was.

I tried to wax casual, no matter how frightened I really felt. "Hey, that *is* Gentian, isn't it?" I asked her.

She patted his face with her free hand. "Yep." She used the same hand to swipe at her nose and her cheeks. It was odd to see someone crying and threatening you at the same time.

"What's he doing now?" I asked her, which is the insider's way of asking how far along he was in his training.

"Oh, Robin, you should see. He's doing his twos."

"His twos!" I said. She was referring to his tempi changes, flying changes of lead at every second canter stride. It was impressive and I was duly awed. "God," I said, "that's wonderful."

The gun never wavered, though.

"You see what I mean?" She tried to convince me about the tale that she'd told. "I could never have afforded a horse like this on my own, and then Wolf came along, and now here I am, doing my twos."

"Who do you work with down here?" I mean, even though Marilee was a very good rider, twos, or even flying changes, aren't something you can easily teach yourself.

"Wolf. He—"

But before she could finish answering, I had— you guessed it—another *turista* twinge. "Wait, Marilee," I said, backing away in the general direction of the bathroom that I'd been to on my first visit to the place. "I have to—"

"Robin, you can't do this," she shrieked. "I have a gun on you."

"I know, but see, I have to go in the worst way, Marilee," I said, doubling over now with the cramping need to hit the bathroom pronto. "I'll just—"

Evidently she thought I was leaving in order to blow the whistle on her and the breeding thing. "I'll shoot," she said, raising the gun a bit higher.

I started unbuttoning, hoping to convince her. But there wasn't time! "You'll have to shoot," I said, not really caring right then, either. "Because I am *not* stopping."

And with that I slammed into the john, pulling at my trousers as I waited for the bullet that would fell me.

Whew on both fronts.

I heard a car drive up and a man's heavily accented voice. Germanically accented. "They know and they're coming and the goddamn cows are out," he said.

"What?" Marilee said. "Aw, no!" Her voice receding as, I guess, she went outside to see.

"We don't have time to deal with it now," the male voice said as it similarly faded. "We must . . ."

I couldn't hear whatever else they might have said, but it was probably about me. I mean, I don't think that Marilee, cows or no cows, was going to forget I was in there.

I sat, hunched over and miserable, thinking that I might have been able to talk Marilee out of killing me, but not Wolf.

He was probably out there now, arguing with her about how to do it. Slowly, he'd probably say. Slowly and painfully. Surely I could count on Marilee to opt for merciful and fast.

However it happened, it would happen soon. It was only a matter of time.

I pulled my trousers up. I figured that if I went out there to face the music, maybe things would go easier for me. Because if I stayed in here, they'd just pepper the whole room with one hail of bullets and—

Just then there was a *c-rrack*.

Oh, no.

Except that it seemed like a warning shot rather than an attack. I mean, nothing had come splintering through the bathroom door.

But this would be a terrible way to die, trapped inside the bathroom. And not just terrible, but ignominious, degrading, the kind of death that would end up in *News of the Weird*.

I burst out of the room. I would stare whatever waited for me, I decided, right in the face.

Except that there was no one out there in the stable except for Gentian, still cross-tied.

I went to the doorway to see where Wolf and Marilee were. And I flinched at what I saw.

Marilee was lying outside on the ground in a pool of blood. My first instinct was to go to her. I beat it down. She was way too still. Wolf had killed her!

My next instinct was to hide. Where? In one of the stalls.

I turned to do that and ran smack into him. For a moment I didn't even realize that. He was hard as stone. I reared back, thinking I'd run into a pillar, and when I saw that it was Wolf, I screamed.

Wolf threw his arms around me, trapping me against his chest. He was trying to get his hand either to my mouth or my neck, I wasn't sure which.

I tried to slam my foot down on his instep, which is what my old gym teacher, Ms. Barr, always said to do. Slam, slam, slam, I went, but I couldn't connect.

And I couldn't get my hands free, either, to gouge at his eyes or, indeed, anything gougeable. But I didn't give up. I squirmed and kicked and fought. I even tried to bite any part of him I could get my teeth near, but I kept getting mouthfuls of fabric. Also, *he* was moving, so my teeth would ache when he wrenched whatever I'd caught hold of away.

I could taste blood, but I think it was my own.

Then something hard came down against my head and everything went black.

CHAPTER 9

I expected to wake up in heaven, but instead, I woke up all scrunched down in the front seat of Wolf's Jaguar roadster. He was inching his way up the driveway. I say inching because there were cows everywhere, and he was trying to avoid having one of them crumple his sleek Jaguar fenders.

I had come to, in fact, with a huge brown heifer bellowing all too near my ear right over the low-slung door of the car.

The good news was that Wolf didn't realize that I *had* come to.

I stayed there in fetal position and pondered my options.

I could jump out and maybe even land on my feet at the pokey rate we were going.

Except that he would catch me.

If he didn't drive after me, he'd run, and his legs were probably twice as long as mine.

So I'd have to be very very smart and . . .

I shut my eyes again, trying to latch onto whatever it was that was teasing my brain. There was a way, there was, if I could just remember it. It had to do with Marilee, Marilee back in Texas. . . .

And then it came to me.

I jerked up before Wolf could register that I had and reached past him before he could even begin to stop me, leaning on the horn for as long as I dared.

"No, you fool," he shouted as I found the door handle and hurled myself out of the Jag.

I didn't land on my feet, but I didn't care, either. I was so pleased that I'd been right about Marilee and the cows.

I mean, it stood to reason that if she used the horn of her pickup as the chuckwagon bell back in Texas, she'd do the very same thing here in Mexico, right?

The answer was the mooing mass of cows surrounding Wolf and his car. I could see Wolf's upraised fist, and I could—though just barely—make out what he was shouting. It was something about having signed my death warrant.

Well, hey. I knew that.

But then he said—or at least I think he did—"I was saving you!"

Saving me, ha! How gullible did he think I was?

And I guess next he'd be saying that he hadn't killed Marilee. Right. The image of her body in that pool of blood came back to knock the tough-guy pose I was trying to assume right out from under me.

Marilee! Something within me was shouting out her name. But I had to get past this sudden spurt of sorrow and save myself.

I scooted back toward the barn, cows swarming past me in the opposite direction, all bent on getting to the spot where they'd heard that horn. God, that had been a neat maneuver on my part.

But perhaps I'd congratulated myself a bit too soon.

Because I heard Wolf's voice again, closer, as though he had nearly caught up to me. "Get down! Get down, or they'll kill you, too," he was saying, trying to confuse me, I suppose.

Except that just then there was the sound I'd heard while I was in the bathroom, that *c-rrack* that had brought down Marilee. Except that the source hadn't been Wolf, directly behind me, but someone somewhere off to my right.

Who?

Someone else with a rifle. An accomplice.

Ernesto?

I could not imagine him shouldering a weapon.

But I was in the barn now, no longer a target. But the door had no bolt.

And forget the door anyway, because Gentian was wild-eyed, trapped, as it were, in the cross ties. I paused, wondering if I ought to take his tack off and free him, but before I could complete the thought, I heard the *c-rrack* sound yet again.

So it couldn't be an accomplice to Wolf because who else could they be shooting at? At Wolf. Wolf, like me, was a target.

But a little voice said, Naw. This was being done so I'd *think* Wolf was a target. Wolf was after me, wasn't he?

So why hide in the barn, where, sooner or later, Wolf and his cohort would find me, when I could be out of here for real. And unless Wolf had some incredibly superfast way of catching a horse and saddling up, he wouldn't be able to follow me, either.

I went toward Gentian, who was tugging this way and that at the ties.

I pulled at the stirrups to bring them down on the leathers and then I undid the ties. Marilee had put the halter on over his bridle, and I took the halter off.

I looked at the entryway and figured that, crouched over, I could make it out on Gentian's back without decapitating myself.

Then I tried to swing myself up to get on him.

But of course, he was so very tall that, even now, in a life-and-death situation, I wasn't going to be able to do it. I always used a mounting block at home. I cursed the fact that I did that now.

I looked around for something to use—a concrete block, a ladder, anything.

But then I heard the door I'd come through groaning shut and suddenly Wolf was there. He'd sealed off the only exit that I knew about.

"Stay away from me," I said, kind of turning Gentian sideways and using his huge body as a shield.

"I'm not going to hurt you, you dunce." He was half whispering now. "I'm trying to get you out of here."

"You killed Marilee," I said, surprised by the way my voice was pitched—way up there in the Minnie Mouse register.

"I didn't," he said. "Someone out there fired the shot. With a rifle."

"Right. One of your friends."

"They killed Marilee," he said. "They are trying to kill me, too."

"Why?" I asked. "Why would they?"

"Because I protected Sturmgeist," he said. "Now come on. Give me the horse. We can ride out together."

"No."

"They were going to kill Sturmgeist," he said, reaching toward Gentian. "I stopped them. That is why they killed—"

"Oh, right," I interrupted, pulling Gentian back toward myself. "How dumb do you think I am? Like they'd kill the goose that laid the golden egg."

It was his turn to talk. I waited and nothing was said. I poked my face around the horse and saw that Wolf had turned his back to me.

His shoulders were shaking. I realized that he couldn't talk, because he was sobbing. "Marilee," he choked out finally. "My sweet Marilee."

I looked at those shoulders and I knew that he wasn't putting on an act. He was heartbroken. And hadn't Marilee, just before she died, said he'd done something brave? I stepped toward him and tapped him on the back.

He turned, his face contorted with grief.

"Okay," I said. "Okay"—my voice sinking into its normal range. "I believe you, Wolf," I said, handing over Gentian's reins.

He made a bridge with his hands, and I stepped into it and let him lift me up so that I could swing a leg over and lower myself into the saddle. Then, as if it took no effort at all, he put his foot in the stirrup and mounted behind me. Or tried to.

The saddle was too small for both of us. He let

me have it and moved back behind it, right onto the horse's back.

Gentian freaked and acted as though he was about to buck.

The ceiling of the barn wasn't high enough for that. I thought briefly that if we didn't both get catapulted off, we'd be plastered up against the roof as if someone had painted us there.

So Wolf and I both slithered cautiously over the horse's side lest we upset him and find ourselves thus launched.

Our feet hit the ground in unison.

But meanwhile, I had the sense that a huge invisible clock was ticking off the seconds and the minutes. Because the rifleman had to be closing in, coming nearer to the barn.

Wolf undid the girth and took the saddle off, tossing it down the way Marilee had tossed Lola's saddle that day so long ago at the show.

I think that's how sad things come to you, kind of unpredictably, in little waves.

I would have said something about Marilee at that point, but Wolf didn't seem to be in a talking mood. He vaulted soundlessly up onto the horse and sat there, settling, staring down at Gentian's withers as if the future were written there.

I held my breath, waiting, as he was waiting, to see how the horse would react.

Nothing. That was a relief.

"Come," Wolf said, bending down and extending his arm. I took hold of it, and he managed, with an extraordinary show of strength, to lift me high enough that I could scramble onto Gentian's back right in front of him. It wasn't graceful, but hey, I was there.

Once again we waited to see how the horse would feel about this.

He was fine.

"Listen," I said, "there's another problem. See, I don't ride bareback ever, and I don't think I can—" But before I could finish the sentence, he pushed me down, so that I was practically eating the horse's mane.

Then he shifted his weight and I felt the horse's front end turn toward—I peeked to see what—an open doorway down the aisle side.

It had the same low clearance as the door Wolf had closed. Still, I knew that with both of us bent forward this way, we could make it.

But there were other things to worry about. It was a people door, way narrower than the first. I cringed, thinking that our knees would get knocked or maybe even shattered against the doorjamb on the way out. And of course I hoped our assailant wouldn't be waiting outside to shoot us at point-blank range.

Gentian stood stock-still, waiting for a command.

I expected us to move off at a walk, walk through the doorway, at least. But no. I felt Wolf kind of bearing down with his seat and then *boom*.

Gentian exploded forward, halt to gallop, with no gait in between, a burst of equine force that just carried both of us with it.

I didn't even have time to scream, which I probably would have done at the thought of hurtling full speed through that narrow door. It was like be-

ing shot from a cannon, *boom,* moving full speed
from the relative darkness of the barn into an as-
sault of light.

Gentian acted as though the cows weren't there,
and they did prove to be remarkably swift when it
came to getting out of his way. Those cows absolutely broke speed and agility records scattering. It
was like entering some life-size Gary Larson cartoon, except that I couldn't think of a worthy cap-
tion.

And then we were beyond the cows, heading
toward what I hoped was an open gate to the coun-
tryside beyond.

But meanwhile, practical considerations forced
themselves to the fore. Like staying on the horse.

It felt very slippery, sitting right down on the
horse's back like that, even though I was more or
less held in place by Wolf, who seemed secure. I
can't understand why anyone rides bareback.

But just about the time that my mind fell back
into its normal meandering pattern, another re-
sounding *c-rrack* filled the air. Then another, and
another, and the next thing I knew, Wolf's weight
was bearing down on me.

"You're hit, aren't you?" I screamed.

"I am fine," he said. "Grab mane. There is a wall
ahead."

"A wa—" But we were over it. I would have fallen
off for sure had Wolf's body not wishboned itself
around me. I heard Gentian snorting as if he were
having a good old time.

Another *c-rrack* and something to the right of us
made a great splintering sound. I felt Wolf shake,

but it turned out he was laughing. "Ba-ad shot," he said.

I closed my eyes and listened for the sound of the next shot. I think I was waiting, too, for the bullet that would sear right through my flesh.

Before I could say anything back, he cautioned me to "grab mane" again. The wall in front of us seemed tiny compared with the last.

Gentian poised himself momentarily and then arched his body over the jump.

We riders both slid backward with his hesitation and then forward as he jumped. Gentian pecked on landing beneath our sudden shift of weight. For a moment I thought for sure the horse would fall. But he didn't, he recovered and even gave a little playful head toss as he did as if to say, "Hey, I made that, guys!"

There was another *crack*, but it seemed weak compared with the others we had heard, as though the triggerman were far off in the distance now.

Wolf was breathing hard, breathing raggedly. He was leaning against me completely now.

"To the mountains," he said. "We will not be safe in San Mi—" He didn't finish.

I held my breath, knowing, I think, what that labored pause meant. And then Wolf fell heavily to the side, dragging me off the horse's back with him.

At the very last minute I grabbed the reins and hung on for dear life. They looped over Gentian's head, but his motion pulled him—and me—forward. I ran alongside, and he slowed as I tugged backward, shouting, "Whoa, whoa, whoa boy."

I got him stopped and looked back. Wolf was sprawled maybe a hundred feet behind the horse and me. I could see his hand twitching, but otherwise he was completely still. It was horrible, that erratic twitch, as if he were beckoning me to join him.

I started back toward him, leading Gentian, but Gentian kept stopping, planting his legs as though they had no joints, and snorting at the sight of Wolf there on the ground.

You know how silly horses are when anything looks out of the ordinary. And Gentian had never seen Wolf—who had trained him, probably—sprawled out like that.

"Come on . . ." I kept trying to soothe him, move him closer to Wolf. I considered just letting go of the horse, but if he ran away, where would I be?

So it took long, long minutes before I was able to kneel at Wolf's side.

And he wasn't dead. He was breathing, lying on his side, blood bubbling at his mouth.

Gentian was still wary, but he stood there.

But how would I get Wolf back to San Miguel?

The answer was clear: I couldn't. I would have to bring help back to him. I looked for some way to remember the terrain, but it all looked pretty much the same: cactus, some mesquite. Rocks and gritty soil.

"Fa . . ." Wolf said, and then began coughing. More blood.

"Don't talk," I ordered him. "Which way is San Miguel?"

"Moun . . ."

"Forget the mountains," I screamed at him. "You need a doctor. You . . ."

And he began convulsing; his eyes rolled back, blood pulsing at his mouth and rolling down his chin.

Gentian lost it, leaping backward about twenty or thirty feet, and taking me along with him. In a way, if I hadn't had the horse to calm, I'd have been panicky, too. As it was, Gentian's behavior diluted the horror that was taking place.

Because Wolf continued jerking around on the ground, as though something inside him was struggling to get out.

And Gentian continued yanking my arms—because I had hold of the reins with both hands now—nearly out of their sockets.

"Easy, easy," I kept saying, mad and at the same time grateful for having to worry about the horse when a human being yards away was probably dying.

Given his druthers, Gentian would have run back toward the barn and the guy with the rifle. I continued trying to persuade him to stay. I continued chanting, "Easy," and in an odd way, it worked on me as much as it did the horse.

And thank God. I mean, Gentian was the getaway car, right? So I continued crooning, rubbing his neck, trying to get closer to Wolf.

He still wasn't convinced, though he was merely prancing now. "Shhh, shhh," I tried. And then as if some switch had been thrown, he stopped and was calm.

I knew and didn't want to know what it meant. And then I turned to see if I was right.

Yes. Wolf's own movement had stopped. He was spread out on the ground, still as could be.

I approached, and this time Gentian didn't give me any trouble.

I felt the tears again, tears of—what? Admiration.

How long had Wolf ridden with the life leaking out of him? Because I think he'd been hit very early on. I think the first time he'd assured me he was fine, he had, in fact, taken the bullet that claimed him.

God, how incredibly skilled a rider he had been. I swallowed, wondering if I'd live to tell anyone the tale.

I saw the corner of a sheet of paper flapping from Wolf's pocket. I pulled it free. It was addressed to someone in Argentina on La Conexión stationery and it didn't pull any punches:

MOVE STURMGEIST TO SAFETY IMMEDIATELY OR HE WILL BE KILLED.

That was the brave and wonderful thing that Marilee had mentioned, I'll bet. The brave and wonderful thing that got both her and Wolfgang killed.

And then, as though some fierce part of Wolf's spirit had suddenly fused itself with mine, I thought, I will make it, goddamn it! For Wolf and for Marilee and, not least of all, for Jeet!

* * *

I looked around for a slope sufficient to let me climb back on the horse. I found one. Then, once aboard, I tried to move off slowly. There was no Wolf now to keep me in place.

Gentian's walk was big, and I moved around on his back as if I were on some kiddy ride at an amusement park. But walking wasn't going to cut it, not if I hoped to make it anywhere, whether to the mountains or back to town.

But would I make it? Bareback, I just didn't see how. I mean, I'm not the world's worst rider, but saddles offer an amazing amount of stability. Maybe not even saddles, maybe stirrups do. Without them, I felt loose as a goose, which, under the circumstances, meant doomed.

Except that I knew I could reasonably expect to survive a fall, whereas I didn't think my odds were quite as good with a gunshot. At least I'd had experience with falling, a track record, as it were.

So I screwed up my courage and tipped my pelvis forward to speed Gentian up.

Oy. The horse took two big, bouncy trot steps and I pulled him up.

Now I knew why Wolf had gone from a halt to a gallop without any in-between. I mean, we're talking major bounce. And of course, anticipating it would make me even tighter, so that I ended up bouncing even more. So I had to forget trotting altogether.

I gathered up the reins and a good bit of mane along with them, hunkered down for a push, and so as not to leave any doubt in Gentian's mind, yelled like someone in a Western movie, "Yee-haw."

Look, don't write me letters about classical technique. There was a maniac with a gun out there!

And anyway, Gentian knew what he was being asked to do. He responded to the idea with glee. And something—whether centrifugal force or the patron saint of bareback maidens—kept me in position as we sped along.

I got used to the motion, used to the sound, used to the ground being gobbled up beneath the horse's long, sure stride. I felt confident, high, sure that we were going to make it after all.

Eventually I spotted a road up ahead. I knew that slowing down was going to hurt. I sat upright, tried to make myself soft in the loins so that I'd bounce a lot less, and through clenched teeth, said, "Whoa."

Maybe I was numb, but it wasn't as bad as I'd feared. In fact, Gentian stopped so abruptly that there was one big ouch instead of several long little ones. I'd learned to count my blessings.

I slid off and felt the sting of the ground on the soles of my feet. I hoped that I would still be able to stand.

Indeed, my knees buckled, and my first few steps were very iffy, but I managed. I was really going to hurt in the morning, though, and possibly several mornings hence.

That's better than never hurting again, I thought. Like Marilee, and Wolf, and Felipe, too.

I took the reins over the horse's head, and then, with Gentian at my side, I moved on in what I hoped was the direction of San Miguel de Allende.

CHAPTER 10

My first thought was that I should stop the first passing motorist, but my next thought was that said motorist could be the killer.

Except that didn't make much sense.

The killer hadn't been in a car—at least, I didn't think so.

Who could the killer be?

The person I most despised in San Miguel was Ernesto, so my suspicions tended to settle there. Oh, true, I couldn't imagine him actually pulling the trigger on his own, but he'd have his minions.

Of course, if this were a movie, it would be the person I liked the best. Ramon Pedras.

But I didn't think so, not really.

Ernesto. And a man in his employ. They could be barreling down the highway toward me right now.

Except that nobody came down the highway. Not a soul. It was as though San Miguel were under some sort of curfew, or else that the whole town had been evacuated for some reason. Maybe it was that feast day the woman in Milagro's kitchen had mentioned. Had she told me the name?

St. Whoever. I giggled at the thought.

Obviously, I was tiring, and it was taking its toll. Even so, I kept on going. I had no choice.

I began to consider the possibility that I was heading the wrong way, but I ruled that out. The reason for that was that the sun was setting and I could see a sort of glow up ahead, a glow that could only be San Miguel.

And meanwhile I kept trying, as I walked, to reason the whole thing out. For instance, why would Ernesto Quinto be involved in some horse-breeding scam?

Then I remembered whatever it was Jeet had said about Ernesto's cousin. I think it was cousin. That he was a world-class equestrian. Rode jumpers, I think. So Ernesto knew something about the horse world, about how much money these horses could bring.

And anyway, I'd *seen* the very man at Milagro, so he damn well was involved.

And Pedras, even laissez faire as he was, would have to pay some attention, ferret that information out, when he saw the bodies of Wolf and Marilee.

The proof.

I shivered, thinking that I'd managed to reduce them to that. Then I tried to steer away from the thought by picturing those dozens and dozens of Sturmgeist babies out there in Milagro's fields.

Except with all these look-alikes, things at a show were going to get very complicated. And with all of them equally talented—which is what I'd assume—plain old riding skill was going to count for a lot more.

It was kind of like a photography class that Jeet

told me about, where everyone had to put away
their expensive Nikons and their big long lenses
and go out on the street with Instamatics. The leveler.

Inadvertently, that's what Marilee and Wolf had
produced—a leveler for all of these people who
tried to outbuy each other into the ribbons.

Interesting.

Gentian, who had been walking alongside me
quite pleasantly, began to lag behind. I clucked to
him and tried to urge him on, but no go. He took a
few steps, yes, but they were very grudgingly
taken. I halted to see what was afoot, thinking,
Please don't let him be lame, please, please.

Because under the circumstances, lame or not,
he was going to have to keep going. Like that poor
horse in *Fiddler on the Roof.*

Gentian stopped gratefully, groaned, and camped
his hind legs out behind him. So he wasn't lame.
No. He took what must have been a ten-minute
pee.

Which reminded me—as I felt for my fanny pack
and found it still in place even after all I'd been
through—that it had been a good long while since
I'd had to go to the bathroom myself.

See? Things are never *totally* bad.

And meanwhile, the glow of San Miguel was getting comfortingly near. San Miguel and—my heart-
strings tugged—Jeet. I hadn't dared think about
him again until now.

Jeet is all right, he's all right, they wouldn't dare
murder him, I told myself. And despite what had

happened to Marilee and Wolf, I believed it was true. I mean, you could argue that Marilee had been a U.S. citizen, too, but she was in Mexico, involved in something illegal, and you've probably seen enough movies to know that crooks and criminals are always killing each other.

Maybe, I thought, forcing myself to look on the bright side, maybe Jeet had only left me for another woman or something.

Gentian had finished taking his whiz.

It had grown pretty dark in the meanwhile. Not that that's how long he'd peed, it was just the end of the day when the light died quickly. Actual total darkness would be upon us in, say, fifteen minutes or so.

I guess my eyes were on the glow of San Miguel, but fortunately, Gentian's were sighted lower. Because we were on the edge of a cliff, and I'd have walked right off if Gentian hadn't ground to a halt and snorted at the brink.

I hadn't been wrong about the glow. Oh, no. The lights of the town were there all right, responsible for the glow that I'd been moving toward. But intervening was a monstrously huge canyon, and you're right, it was the canyon where Ernesto's house had been built.

In fact, I could see the house there on the cliff in the gathering gloom.

So no wonder there hadn't been the stream of traffic I'd anticipated. I'd been on a lonely road. The road to the lovers' lane.

Briefly, I thought about Ernesto's telescope, but it seemed too coincidental, even for me, to assume that he would had been looking out of it right that very minute. Also, there were no lovers here as yet and he probably had the tryst schedule down pat.

Except that I was wrong.

He was there, looking for me.

Oh, I didn't see him. It was way too far. But I heard the sound of his big glass wall of window whooshing open. That carried across the chasm, and it was followed by Ernesto's own rasping voice. "There!" he said. "There she is!"

I had to backtrack, and quickly, but first I had to get on the horse. I managed to feel around and find another place where I could position myself sufficiently higher than Gentian to drop aboard.

He was a good boy, still as a statue while I did this, too.

But as I did I thought, Great. You're not only riding some incredibly enormous horse bareback through rock-strewn, cactus-laden country, but you're going to be doing it in pitch-dark night. For my own peace of mind, I consciously omitted the part about Ernesto coming in search of me. And you know how effective that was: will the jury please disregard . . .

Anyway, I proceeded, because what alternative was there?

Except that the aches I'd predicted for the following day had already settled in. Even as the horse walked, my whole body creaked and moaned with the motion. And walking wasn't going to cut it, not under these circumstances.

But how could I ask Gentian to go faster when

he'd probably end up impaling himself on one of those cactus trees I told you about—the kind that look like upside-down umbrellas?

And anyway, the way my arms were aching, I wouldn't have any control. And if I got this horse really rolling, where would he be likely to go? Right back to Milagro, where Marilee's corpse lay waiting. And we'd pass poor Wolf along the way. What would that achieve?

The only answer was to ignore these thoughts and look on the bright side. Like, when I got back to the main road. I could gallop in relative safety along the shoulder. What was more, I could see headlights from a long way off. I could therefore make time on the way back to San Miguel and hide myself in the darkness whenever Ernesto and his boys came out to troll for me along the highway.

With that in mind, I closed my legs on the horse's sides, one a tad ahead of the other to ask for canter.

My legs were weak. Gentian began to trot, and surprisingly, my body was so wholly worn out that I was able to sit there in a boneless sort of way, so boneless that I didn't bounce at all. It was a good thing, too, because if my seat hadn't been so deep, I'd have surely gone off.

Because Gentian was weaving this way and that, seeing cacti and rocks that I, given the depth of night upon us now, couldn't. Either that or he was trying, in a subtle way, to knock me off.

I preferred to think it was the former. That he was dodging obstacles as we went. Horses are not given to great subtlety, for one thing.

I heard his hooves clack against a harder surface

and I knew we'd hit it—the road. The real road, the one to San Miguel. I slowed him to a walk again and guided him to what had to be the highway's edge.

And I wondered, What happened to the moon that was shining so prettily just the other night? Where is it? But moon or no moon, tired or not tired, I knew what I had to do now.

Okay.

And I bent forward, hollered, and took off flying, my fingers dug into Gentian's mane and my body tucked as close to his as I could get it.

His enthusiasm had waned, as if he were thinking, This is getting old. But he didn't think to disobey and galloped on.

The rhythmic sound of his hooves on the dirt sounded like a lullaby, but of course I wasn't about to fall asleep. Oh, no. I had a husband to save, maybe, although the thought of Jeet in the hands of the enemy seemed increasingly remote. But I had murderers to turn in, for sure.

I could feel my last residue of strength waning away. I tried to cheer myself as before, by tuning into the sound. *Ba-da-dump, Ba-da-dump*, I thought, then, Half a league, half a league. Jeet would have liked that. What was it? Iambic tetrameter or something, the rhythm of a horse at the gallop.

But the rhythm stopped, and jarringly, too. I felt something roll under the horse's left front hoof, felt his left shoulder go down. There was a slow-mo quality to it.

He'd stumbled, finally as tired as I.

And then the action speeded dramatically. I was airborne, the reins and Gentian's mane jerked rudely out of my hands.

I audibly hit the ground. The sound? I actually saw it as a word in a cartoon balloon rising over my head: SPLAT!

CHAPTER 11

I opened my eyes and found myself staring up at Jeet, who was on his knees beside me. I blinked, thinking I was dreaming, but his image survived. "Oh," I said, straining to reach up and throw my arms around him.

"You'd better not move," he said. "You were unconscious. Something might be broken."

"I thought you were kidnapped," I said, paying absolutely no attention to his advice. "And nothing's broken, look." I knelt in front of him and wiggled and jiggled my limbs.

Then I realized what enabled him to see me was the beam of a headlight. The Fiesta, I thought, but no. It was too big, too long. It was Ernesto's car, the Bentley, and standing alongside it was Ernesto himself.

"Oh, no," I said to Jeet. "You *were* kidnapped. And he still has you. And now he has me, too. Oh, no."

"Robin, what are you talking about? Ernesto and I have been trying to find you. It was just by luck that he happened to be scanning the ridge when you appeared."

"Luck, my foot," I said, standing upright now.

Jeet was standing, too, and Ernesto was moving toward us. "He's behind all this," I said, pointing. "Ernesto. He's the one who . . ." But where should I begin?

"Robin." Jeet stroked my arm. "You've had a bad knock on your head and you're—"

"Jeet, no!" I pulled away from Ernesto, and Jeet actually apologized to him, saying that I wasn't myself.

"You bet I'm not myself," I said. "I've just seen two people murdered. No, three. Three, if you count Felipe."

Jeet was still trying to persuade me things were hunky-dory. "Jeet," I said, "do you deny that you were kidnapped?"

"Kidnapped!" he said. "Well, I guess you could say I was if you count that crazed gourmet who took umbrage at what I'd said about the *chile rellenos*. But you know, he was right. His own *were* better. He had used a corn-based batter, almost a fritterlike substa—"

'Stop," I said. "Are you telling me that while I thought you'd been kidnapped, you were actually sitting down with somebody eating *chile rellenos*? That's why you abandoned me at *comida corrida*? So you could go off and eat something else?"

"I didn't know you'd thought I was kidnapped," Jeet said. "It's a pretty wild thing to think. And anyway, I left a note with the waiter . . . oh."

"Oh, what?"

"Well, actually I planned to leave a note, but the pen wouldn't write and this man was driving me up a wall and finally I said . . ."

"Yes?" This wasn't like Jeet. He's usually pretty direct.

He sucked some night air into his lungs. "Well, I did kind of say—jokingly—'Tell my wife I've been kidnapped by a crazed gourmet.'" He looked sheepish.

I could only stare.

Which made him go on. "Actually, I don't think I said 'crazed gourmet.' I think I said the man's name. Whatever it was. I don't really remember now."

"But you did say kidnapped."

"Jokingly. Yes."

"Oh God," I said. But hey. At least it meant I wasn't crazy. "Where's Gentian?"

Jeet looked puzzled.

"The horse."

"He was gone when we pulled up. I guess he took off," Jeet said. "Come on. Ernesto will drive us back to his place."

"Jeet," I screamed, "there are two dead people back there. Two dead people lying in the road."

That wasn't exactly where they were, but I wanted to make my point. Except that Jeet looked at me, like, oh-the-old-dead-people-in-the-road story, and I realized I was shrieking again.

"Jeet, I'm not brain-damaged, I'm not. There are dead people, Wolf and Marilee, and there is a Sturmgeist baby, Gentian, a horse that's worth beaucoup bucks wandering around the highway here at night, and there are other Sturmgeist babies at Milagro. . . ."

Jeet looked stricken. Really worried about me. And I guess the words didn't make much sense if you didn't know who and what the principals were, who the proper nouns referred to. In fact, it probably sounded like gibberish.

"I want the police. I want the police," I said, an inch away from stamping my foot for emphasis.

Ernesto came forward with a cellular phone in his hand. "I have just spoken to the police," he said. "They have picked up the horse in a van and taken him back to the owner."

"The owner is dead, Ernesto."

"The horse," he insisted, "has been returned."

"Jeet," I said, "this is a lie. He's in this up to his eyeballs." I tried to sound as sane as possible, but I was getting shrill again.

Except that, wouldn't *you* be? "Look"—I compromised—"just let me talk to the police myself."

Jeet and Ernesto conferred. Then Jeet said, "I'll take you to the police after the doctor has looked at you and I won't take no for an answer."

"Fine. Take me to the doctor."

"Ernesto is calling a doctor on his car phone and we are taking you to Ernesto's, where you will be examined and treated. The doctor will meet us there."

I wanted to warn him, say, Jeet, you're playing right into his trap, but I knew it wouldn't get me anywhere. Jeet obviously thought I was talking derangedly and that was why he was speaking in stilted sentences without a single contraction. So instead I said, "And then after that you'll take me to the police? You promise?"

"Then I will take you, I swear, to the police."

"Okay." I lurched toward Ernesto's car. I was aching all over. I felt as if the marrow had been vacu-
umed from my bones.

All the way back into San Miguel I peered out
into the blackness, scanning for Gentian, because I
didn't believe a thing Ernesto said. Of course, the
horse probably *had* long since gone back home. And
he was a savvy horse, so he probably didn't have
any trouble at all negotiating in the dark.

But what about Jeet and me? I was the only one
who knew the danger we were in. What could
Ernesto be planning to do with us? And then it occurred to me:

Nothing.

As long as he could keep me quiet until whoever
got rid of the bodies back at Milagro, he was home
free. Because if my own husband wouldn't believe
me, who would? Just by having carried on about
Jeet being kidnapped, I'd more or less destroyed
my credibility with Officer Pedras. And besides,
Pedras was afraid of Ernesto Quinto anyway.

I started to cry, the benefit of this being that my
husband took me in his arms. "Shhhh," he said. "It
will all turn out okay."

"How could you leave me in that restaurant?" I
sniveled.

Jeet laughed. "I didn't think you were ever coming out of that bathroom. And the crazed gourmet
was pretty darned insistent. And anyway, I did tell
the waiter his name, so I thought you'd be coming
along."

"And how would I do that?"

"You'd look in the *Juarde*." That telephone book I mentioned before, the one that lists Americans.

"He was American?"

"Canadian or something. I don't remember. But the point is, I figured I might as well go and you could join me as soon as you could."

"Well, when I didn't come, weren't you worried?"

"Unlike you, Robin, I did *not* come to the worst possible conclusion. I just figured you'd already had something planned for that afternoon. But later, when you didn't show up, I called Ernesto and he helped me call around."

"Did you have him call the police?"

"I assume he did."

Right. "Did you have him call Milàgro?"

"I couldn't remember the name of the place," Jeet admitted. "I told him some big dressage place."

"And did he know where you meant?"

"I don't know. He mentioned Hans Bell. Isn't that the guy you interviewed?"

"Yeah, but that wasn't where I was."

He kissed my forehead. "All's well that ends well," he said.

"Yeah, but this hasn't ended."

The doctor was pulling up as we arrived. He seemed pleasant enough. He did the standard things, you know, made me move this and that, and shone a light into my eyes and made me follow it.

"She is fine," he told my husband and Ernesto.

Jeet looked cheered, but Ernesto, I swear, was disappointed. Still, he recovered. "We will dine together, all of us," he said, including, with a wave of his hand, the doc. Then, to me: "You would, perhaps, care to perform your toilette."

Had he heard about my diarrhea?

"Well, actually," I said, reaching for my fanny pack, "I've been fine. . . ." Even though I hadn't needed it, I was glad the little bottle of *turista* medicine had survived the whole ordeal intact. Just in case.

"Good idea," Jeet interrupted, kind of steering me away.

"I will have someone show you upstairs," Ernesto said. He went over to a wall and pressed something, and a maid in a uniform appeared.

As if we were accustomed to such things, Jeet and I followed her up a huge, wide floating spiral staircase and down a lengthy corridor.

The minute she left us, I started searching for the phone, but can you believe this? All this luxury and there was not a telephone to be had.

"Robin, Robin, relax," Jeet kept saying, as though placing a call marked another retreat from sanity.

Which made me realize—like one of those really canny nut cases—that if I didn't control myself, he'd call the doctor up here and they'd tranq me. And then where would I be?

"Okay," I said. And then I glanced into a huge gilt-edged mirror and almost screamed when I saw myself.

"Jeet!" I said, staring at my tattered shirt, my utterly begrimed face and neck and arms.

"Nothing that can't be fixed." He stood beside me, crisp and clean as could be, and smiled.

Just then a door popped open and the maid appeared, indicating a deep, steaming tub full of bubbles. A wonderful lavender scent issued from the room.

The maid smiled and I moved toward her as though she'd hypnotized me.

I guess I'm easy.

I mean, I would hate to be tortured, but you could probably bribe me with luxury, indeed, with far less luxury than this.

I stepped inside the bath chamber, let the moist, warm air close around me.

And it got even better. The maid showed me a thick terry-cloth bathrobe and hung it on a kind of person-shaped silhouette. Then she made a show of plugging the silhouette thing in.

It was—get this—a bathrobe warmer. Pretty snazzy.

I stripped and crawled into the bubbles. She scooped up my dirty clothes and disappeared. Meanwhile Jeet came in.

"They just brought our suitcases over from the hotel," he said. "So you'll have something to change into."

"Mmmm," I answered, steeping.

I was thinking, Yeah, maybe I did imagine everything. Maybe I'm just as hysterical as people always think. Maybe all of this had been a dream, like on *Dallas* that year.

I shut my eyes, and when I opened them, Jeet was smiling down at me.

"You're so pink," he said.

"Racist," I teased him. "Come on," I tried. "This tub is big enough for two."

"I'd love to," he said, "but we have a waiting gourmet."

"Oh, right," I scoffed. "Some gourmet."

"Meaning?"

"Never mind."

"Robin?"

"You don't want to know." I carefully checked him out. His stance, the expression on his face. I knew Jeet so very well that I could gauge, pretty much, how he'd react to something before it actually happened. Even something as ghastly as having given *turista* medicine to Ernesto while pretending it was a fine liqueur.

"Okay," I decided, and I told him about it.

"You're making this up," Jeet said, but I could see that he was trying hard not to laugh.

"I'm not!" I offered to lay some on Ernesto again so that Jeet could see for himself, but he demurred.

"But what did Ernesto do to deserve such a thing?" he asked.

"He was ogling my breasts," I said. I know, men do that, but he was doing it in an obvious and icky kind of way.

"Who can blame him?" Jeet said.

Before he could say anything more, alas, someone knocked on the outer door. Jeet went off and returned to say that we had to get a move on.

The heated bathrobe, need I say, was heaven and I insisted on staying in it until it cooled off.

My basic black dress was ready and waiting. I slid the *turista* juice into one of its big patch pockets. It made a bulge, but I didn't really care. Maybe

Ernesto would think it was a gun and cease and desist. Meanwhile, I was determined to let Jeet see Ernesto gobbling the stuff.

Ernesto was all greasy charm when we came downstairs. "Oh, Señora Robin, you are flushed," he said, trundling over to me.

"I'm pink from the bath," I said, shrinking away.

"Oh, no," he said, "It is more than that. Come, doctor. Have a look."

I swear, I saw him wink at the doctor, who went scurrying off to get his little black bag.

"Jeet . . . ?" I looked around, but Jeet was examining a tray of cheeses.

The doctor began taking something out of his bag, a flash of silver, it seemed.

A needle?

"Perhaps." The doctor reached for me, caught hold of my arm.

"Let me go," I shouted, pulling away and knocking over a little end table. A crystal bowl shattered at my feet and the cashews that had been in it went flying around the room.

The doctor was still advancing on me, and I was whimpering as I fled.

I heard Ernesto confiding to Jeet as Jeet strode toward me. The word *hysteria* was mentioned at least twice.

The doctor had a bottle in his hand, and I heard him say that whatever it was would be harmless.

"This is for your own good," Jeet said, and he stepped past me to block my way.

The doctor held out a spoonful of whatever elixir.

"A sedative," he said. "Quite mild."

I pulled the doctor close and whispered in his ear. "What would you say if I told you Ernesto Quinto killed three people, or had them killed, and that he was involved in a breeding scam that involved stealing semen from a stallion who was owned by a Nazi in Argentina and—"

"I would say you needed something stronger than what I have given you," the doctor whispered back, fumbling through his bag again.

Jeet and Ernesto were back at the cheese tray, neither of them looking my way.

And before I knew what hit me, the doc had stuck me with a hypodermic. "Now lie down, please," he said pleasantly. "Let the drug do its job."

This drug was doing it. And it was nothing mild. The room was going wavy. I was determined to battle the drug's effect no matter how potent it was.

I imagined myself telling the doctor to contact Officer Ramon Pedras for me, but all that came out was the one word, "Pedras."

For a moment I thought the word meant feet and the notion made me laugh.

Jeet and Ernesto were looking at me now. Ernesto whispered something to Jeet, but the only word I could pick out was "feverish."

"Come on, hon." Jeet took hold of my arm. "Come sit down."

I thought I was already sitting down, but when I looked at my body, Jeet was right, I was standing.

"Pedras," I said. "Please." Surely the doc wasn't in on it, too.

"Ah," Ernesto said. "Ramon Pedras is a rake. He

flirts with all the women. Some of them quite successfully."

I wanted to punch Ernesto in the gut. Especially when I saw the worried look that crossed Jeet's face.

"Love you," I said, but it must have seemed I said it to no one in particular.

"We should leave her," the doctor told Jeet. "Allow her to rest."

I tried to say no with my eyes, but Jeet didn't seem to be picking up on it. He and the others went into another room. I lay there, feeling as though a lead blanket had been dropped over me.

Ramon Pedras. Would Jeet ever think that? That I'd be interested in another man? Because I wouldn't be, couldn't be, didn't ever ever ever want to be. But it must have seemed that way, me shouting out Pedras's name. Still, it was Pedras who would save us. Unless of course he was in on it.

And it looked as though he was the only person I could turn to now. Because even Jeet wouldn't listen to me. It was Pedras or no one who would have to save me, save Jeet, save Gentian and all those handprinted horses. . . .

And the next thing I knew I was inching toward the big wooden front doors. It took an eternity to get there. The voices of the men were still loud in the room beyond, and I knew from their laughter that they'd forgotten me completely.

Pedras, I told myself, opening one of the doors with elaborate caution.

And then I was outside, tumbling down the steps and falling onto the steep San Miguel street.

I tried to focus. It was eerie, like being inside a painting, a painting by De Chirico called *Mystery and Melancholy of a Street*.

Except that the painting felt tilted, as if it were hung crooked on the wall.

You're going downhill, I told myself. Downhill toward the older part of town. Toward Pedras.

And then—again, just as in the painting, there were arches, and there was the shadow of a child at play and everything was sinister, the light too bright and the edges somehow too harsh.

And I was moving down, through the painting, moving from one arch to the next to the next.

A little girl approached me.

"Bimbo?" the little girl said, and I gaped at her, tried to tell her, no, that I was a housewife, the wife of Jeet Vaughan. But then I remembered where I'd seen her before. *"Policía,"* I said. *"Policía."*

She handed me a cellophane-wrapped cake and began to guide me through the streets. I squeezed the cake, but it didn't open.

And then I was in a room with Officer Pedras, and he was opening the package and breaking off a cream-filled something and laughing. "You are very drunk, señora," he was saying, chewing the cake and offering some to me.

"Ernesto Quinto," I said, eating some, too.

Pedras shrugged.

"Yes. Ernesto Quinto has just called me to report your absence. I will take you back to him." He finished the Bimbo.

"No." But I didn't sound terribly convincing.

"Gracias," Pedras told the little girl as he ushered her and me into one of the Volkswagens that served as police cars.

Well, I was in the front seat at least. The little girl sat on my lap until we reached the poorer neighborhood. "Okay, chiquita," Pedras said, helping her out.

We watched her run down a narrow alleyway that disappeared behind some shacks. Pedras got back in the car. "Oh, señora, señora," he said, over and over again all the way back up the hill. "Meeting you has been quite something."

And then I was back at Ernesto's and Ernesto was saying that it was a pity the doctor was gone because clearly I could use some more of the Demerol he had given me.

Demerol! I looked for Pedras, but he, evidently, had already gone.

All things considered, my navigational skills had been pretty darn good. I think I laughed when I thought that.

"I think we'd better keep her close by with us from now on," Ernesto said to Jeet. "In our sight at all times."

And so I sat propped up on one of the sofas beside my husband while he did extensive schmoozing over some hors d'oeuvres.

There were little potatoes rolled in something green, a sauce, and you ate them with toothpicks. I considered the toothpicks as a weapon, but couldn't get my arms to work sufficiently to reach for one.

Then Ernesto stood up and said it was time to pick out dinner. "You can choose your own cut of meat," he told Jeet, gesturing at the staircase that led below. "I have let my staff go," he boasted. "I will prepare the meal myself. It is a feast day," he explained.

St. Whoever, I thought, realizing that they were going down to that freezer with its carcasses.

Jeet looked at me and tried to bow out. "I don't think we should leave Robin here."

"You are right. She can come along," Ernesto said.

"I don't know," Jeet argued, raising me from the sofa and supporting my weight as best he could. "Those stairs."

"Nonsense." Ernesto came and shored up the other side of me. "The movement will be good for her." I guess he thought I'd escape again if he left me alone upstairs, but to tell you the truth, I was all escaped out.

So the three of us, arm in arm, negotiated the stairs; my legs buckled under me and my armpits ached from the strain of more or less hanging from the shoulders of the two men on either side.

But the movement *was* good for me. Ernesto had been right about that. It made everything a little more clear, as though one, maybe two, of the seven veils that wafted between me and total consciousness had been lifted.

I thought it in my best interest, however, not to let this fact be known. I wobbled around the lower level, which was a sort of library-cum-meat-locker, pulling out various volumes.

There were some heavy-duty leather-bound books there.

Ernesto was no doubt feeling nasty. He yanked

one of them off the shelves. "When your wife is feeling better," he said, "she might be interested in this one. It contains the pedigree of a stallion whom she mentioned. Sturmgeist. It is a pity the stallion did not survive. He was never bred, you know."

Hard as it was, I did not react. I continued blundering about. And Jeet, of course, having realized that the anecdote his host was relating was horse-related, would have tuned right out.

Ernesto said a couple more things about Sturmgeist as he wrenched the freezer door open. Air that was cold as a tomb came whooshing out.

"Robin?" Jeet turned to me.

I had sat down on the Oriental carpet just in front of one of the floor-to-ceiling bookshelves.

Ernesto looked at me. "She will be fine. Just leave her there. Come look at some of the cuts of meat I have in here."

Jeet went in behind him.

The cold air continued washing over me—more of it now that I was seated on the floor—and it lifted maybe two more veils.

When the third veil went up, I stood, walked very carefully over to the freezer door, and slammed it shut. It had a nice, solid—maybe even final—sound.

Then I leaned against it and started giggling.

CHAPTER 12

Sometimes I wish I could slap myself around when I get giddy like this. But whenever I think that—I mean actually picture it—I giggle even more.

So I tried to get the picture out of my mind so that I could force myself into a demeanor vaguely resembling—what? Sobriety, I guess.

I mean, there is no question that this doctor stuck me with something that had me flying high.

And so, Your Honor, I imagined myself saying, I didn't realize I had locked them into a freezer.

Except that Jeet was in there, too. If he weren't, it would be so simple. I'd just fly back home to Texas, right?

But he was and so I'd have to figure out a way to get him out, while leaving Ernesto and the doctor—or wait a minute? Was the doctor in there, too? No, I didn't think so. It was just Ernesto and Jeet. So let me see. It would be Jeet out, Ernesto in.

I had to remember that. *Jeet out, Ernesto in. Jeet out, Ernesto in.* I had to get to the American embassy and tell them that: to get Jeet out, but leave Ernesto in.

And there is an American embassy office in San Miguel de Allende. I had seen it. It probably wouldn't be open now, but I could wait there until it did open up and then lead the ambassador back to Ernesto's house.

Jeet out, Ernesto in.

I stumbled up the staircase and wobbled toward the big front door and yanked.

The cool night air made me shiver. I couldn't worry about that, though. I rubbed my arms and ventured out onto the narrow sidewalk and started once again down that hill.

I heard footfalls and stopped to listen.

Very soft footfalls, yes, but footfalls nonetheless.

Four-legged footfalls, too.

I blinked and told myself to shape up, but the sound continued. It was coming toward me, and I wasn't imagining it, either.

I ducked into a doorway, pressing myself against the wood as if to burrow into it.

The footfalls came closer, closer, and closer still.

My heart was pounding, and my brain was wholly emerging from its drug-induced fog. Terror will do that, I suppose.

And I must have been clear as a bell right then, because I knew beyond doubt what it was that I was hearing.

Burro feet. Eight of them.

And I was sure, too, that the burros weren't there alone.

They were right beside me now, so close I was sure the man who was with them could hear me breathe. Or could hear my heart, which was tossing itself against my rib cage as if trying to escape from my chest. Ka*boing*, ka*boing*.

The man stopped right in front of me, too.

God, maybe he *had* heard.

Because he reached under his serape and took out—oh, my God—a *pistol*.

So I'd been right about the man with the burros all along! He was in cahoots with Ernesto, and he was coming to Ernesto's, not just to get me, but to get Jeet, too.

I expected him to turn and blast me right then, but he didn't, he just checked the gun over, like making sure it was loaded or something, and then put it away.

Then he took something else out.

A cellular phone. Jeez. Ernesto probably had his cellular, too, inside the freezer with him. No wonder I couldn't find a regular one anywhere in the house.

He dialed while standing maybe a foot and a half away from me, and said, "We're nearly home, old chap," in a clipped British accent.

That's right, a clipped British accent. I nearly fell out of my hiding hole, I was so totally shocked. I mean, there he was, big mustache and sombrero, speaking Brit. It's true that he was light-skinned, but then, a lot of Mexicans are. I had just assumed, what with the outfit and all . . .

But hey. What more proof would you need that this guy, as a tender of burros, was not for real? Pedras should have listened to me!

I held my breath.

He put the phone away, and then he pulled the gun out again.

And before he could take another step, I focused all of my meager energy on one thing: the blow that would knock the pistol right out of his hand.

I brought my arms up very slowly, expecting him—or the burros, at least—to react. Miraculously, they didn't.

And then I clasped my hands. I imagined a wrecking ball swinging closer, closer, closer. And then *crash*, I slammed both of my forearms across the man's so that the gun did, indeed, leap from his grasp and bounce on the cobblestone street.

There was a flash and a bang as the gun went off.

The burros went nuts, swirling around him and me. He was taken wholly unaware, and was reaching out blindly, whether for them, or me, or the weapon, I don't know.

I concentrated on looking for the gun, saw it, reached down and got it, though I narrowly missed getting my hand squashed by one of the burros' feet just as I caught hold of it.

I was fully alert now, and I didn't waste a sec. I aimed the gun at him and said, "In the house."

My own voice—its I-mean-business quality— surprised me.

But I did mean business at that.

Ernesto's front door was still wide-open. I motioned for the burro man to step inside. "You've got this all wrong," he said to me. "I'm with Interpol."

"Right," I said, "and I'm Heather Locklear. You

see those stairs? You just go right down them. I don't want any funny business."

The thing is, the burros had come right inside Ernesto's with us. They seemed delighted, moving around the room and nosing this and that. One of them knocked over a chair.

"You should let me tether the animals outside," the man said, "at least."

"The animals will be fine." Actually, it was probably the most fun they'd ever had. "Now go." What? Would Ernesto bill him for the damages? Maybe take it out of his pay? Interpol. What a joke.

The man sighed and took the stairs. I made him keep going until he was standing right in front of the meat locker.

"Open it," I commanded.

"Oh, come now," he said, "This is a bit—"

"You heard me," I growled, interrupting him and even giving his back a nudge with the barrel of the gun.

He lifted the big chrome latch and visibly started when he saw Ernesto and Jeet inside the freezer. He turned to look at me as though he couldn't believe what a royal bitch I'd turned out to be.

And I loved that part especially.

Then he stepped inside. Ernesto came blustering forward but stopped when he saw the gun.

"That's right," I said. "You stay in there. And you, too," to the burro guy. "But Jeet, you come out."

Jeet worked his way around the two others and came and stood beside me. He looked shell-shocked, his eyes big and round and his hair kind of tousled.

"Back up as far as you can go," I told the two

men, and felt the oddest twinge of satisfaction when they did so in yes-ma'am fashion.

"Robin, hon," Jeet said, but I ignored him until I'd slammed the freezer door shut and watched the latch drop into place.

"Phew," I said, lowering the gun.

"My God, Robin," Jeet said, "this is too much. Way too much. Ernesto is going to have a heart attack or something and I just might join him. At the very least he's going to sue our ass. He won't have any trouble, either. I mean, he can have the world's worst lawyer and still end up taking everything we own. The farm, the horses . . ."

He seemed angry.

"What do you mean?" I asked him. "I am a heroine here. I told you, Jeet, three people are dead already. We'd have made five."

"Robin, nobody's out to kill us. I don't know what's gotten into you, but you're . . . paranoid."

"Paranoid! Jeet, do you think I just go around idly locking diplomats into freezers? I mean, do I?"

"Until tonight, no," he said, "but—"

"Jeet, trust me. Please. There is a situation here. You have to at least believe that there is a situation."

"Oh, I believe *that* all right," he said. "I just don't know what it is."

"Look," I said. "That doctor pumped me full of Demerol. Worst-case scenario, we can use that as an excuse."

"But I'm out here with you," he said.

"And I've got a gun."

He looked at it as if for the first time. "Oh, God, Robin, put that thing down."

"I will." And I dropped it into my other dress pocket.

Jeet began looking around the room, feeling behind things.

"What are you doing?" I asked him.

"I'm looking for a thermostat for that freezer. Just on the off chance that you're wrong."

"Is that it?" I gestured at a box of some kind on the wall beside the door. Jeet looked inside it, turned something, and calmed down.

"Okay," he said, "for right now."

"Did you turn it off?"

"The cold, yes. And I turned the one for heat up."

"So they'll be nice and cozy," I said.

I went over to the bookshelf and took the leather-bound volume that Ernesto had taunted me with earlier. I flipped through it and found the Sturm-geist pedigree that he'd talked about.

"It all involves this stallion," I began. "They've been stealing semen from him and impregnating mares and they have a crop of two- or three-year-olds out there that is not to be believed. I mean . . ." Even as I was explaining, I realized I was being swept away by the horse part, which would be the part of least interest to Jeet.

"Get to the point, Robin."

"This *is* the point. They have several fields full of horses that are worth like thirty, forty thou apiece and they're all stolen, more or less. That is, the semen that produced them was stolen and—"

There was a loud crash upstairs. I tried to continue talking, but Jeet waved me quiet. "Someone's upstairs," he mouthed.

"Oh, it's just the burros." I laughed.

"Oh God," he said. "Say you're joking."

"All right, I'm joking, but listen. They were going to kill Sturmgeist. His son was going to stand the stallion, which would make their crop of foals less valuable. So they decided to kill the stallion—"

He interrupted me. "That doesn't make any sense. Why kill the goose that laid the golden egg?"

Isn't it amazing how this little—what is it, an Aesop fable?—fable has gotten around?

There was another crash. Jeet looked up, looked worried again.

"I told you. It's the burros," I said.

"I thought you were joking," he whispered.

"I wasn't. But look, it's okay. Let's go up and see," I said. Then I asked if Ernesto had gotten a phone call while Jeet had been in the freezer.

"A phone call? No. There wasn't any phone."

"Hmmm, that's odd," I said.

The burros had pretty much trashed things upstairs. And Jeet was beside himself. "Robin, we will never extricate ourselves from this mess, we will—"

"We have to call the police," I said. "We can worry about the burros later. Now come on, there has to be a real phone somewhere, and if there isn't one, then one of us will have to go to the police station and get Officer Pedras."

"It won't be me," Jeet said as we followed in the burros' wake. The burros had moved into another of the downstairs rooms. "Look. Can you just get those animals out of here while we sort all this out?" Jeet pleaded. "Is that too much to ask? Things are bad enough as it is without these donkeys roaming around in here."

"Burros."

"Burros, donkeys, mules. I don't care what they are, Robin, I just want them out of this man's home."

He had a point. So together, he and I caught hold of the woven halters that the burros wore and urged them down the front stairs and back into the street. They went very cheerfully.

"Before we go to the police," Jeet said, "I think we have to check . . . you know."

"What?" Did he mean clean up the burro droppings or what? I looked around, but didn't see any.

"The people in the freezer. We have to make sure they're okay."

"Jeet, it's a big freezer. There's air in there. And you turned the heat on."

"No. We have to check."

"Okay," I said resignedly, "but I need to find that gun first, because otherwise, they might get out. I think I left it down there."

"Oh God," Jeet said, "Oh God."

We went back downstairs. Jeet went to the freezer immediately, but I said, "No! Don't you *dare* open it until I find that gun."

A voice above us, like the voice of some evil deity, begged to differ. "You will not be needing your gun," it said. "Soon, in fact, you will not need anything."

This was accompanied by a very slight jangling sound.

It was Hans Bell. And he was wearing his spurs.

CHAPTER 13

He came down the steps very slowly so that the whole thing was very *GQ*: the shiny spurs and the tall leather boots and then the immaculately creased baggy breeches and the great big black gun with a silencer, yet. And then the man himself, Hans Bell, with his slicked-back hair and his fine, aristocratic features.

He complimented me, saying, "You are more intelligent, Señora Vaughan, than I initially surmised."

I didn't thank him. I just glared. "You killed Marilee, didn't you," I said. I didn't put a question mark at the end.

"Sadly, yes."

"And Felipe," I went on. "And Wolf."

"Wolf was a good man at the start," Bell said, "but he had too strong an attachment to the horse. He would have betrayed me in order to save— what? Sturmgeist."

"Why would you kill Sturmgeist anyway?" I asked him. "He was the goose that laid the golden egg." I looked over at Jeet to make sure he was listening.

"Simple economics," Bell said. "We have many Sturmgeist babies now. If Sturmgeist were to stand at stud, they would not be nearly as valuable. But if we killed him . . ."

"Yeah, that's my point," I said. "What then?" There wouldn't be any more after these.

He smiled. Smug. "We have semen stored for yet another crop of foals. Enough for hundreds more."

"And with Sturmgeist dead, the babies would be worth even more money than the first foal crop."

"Exactly."

So it was the old money thing pure and simple. Even if it meant killing people. Even if it meant killing the horse.

"What are you planning to do to us?" Jeet asked him, draping his arm around my shoulder. He sounded unafraid and so brave as to sound casual.

"Oh, I suppose I'll lock you both in the freezer," he said.

"That's original," I said, unable to resist. "And then will you kill us?"

He ignored my question. "Open the latch," he instructed me.

I wondered if he knew Ernesto and the burro man were in there. Or, having come late onto the scene, he'd be taken by surprise. If the latter, then maybe Jeet and I could overpower him while he was registering shock.

I lifted the chrome catch and opened the heavy freezer door, hoping.

But Bell didn't bat an eye.

Ernesto piped right up: "At last," dusting himself off. He was so sweaty that his forehead shone. He'd taken his jacket off and there were huge wet spots on his shirt.

"I'm afraid, Ernesto, my friend, that you will be staying inside with the others," Hans Bell announced. He didn't even make eye contact with Ernesto when he said it.

Ernesto looked stunned. "But we are partners," he protested, staring at the gun.

"We *were* partners," Bell emphasized.

I moved a step closer to Ernesto and comforted him. "Look at the bright side," I said. "At least we won't freeze to death."

Ernesto began to laugh as though grateful for my little joke, but then, almost at once, went into a kind of sputtering choke. He reached toward Bell, his eyes wide.

I turned to see Hans Bell wearing the same facial expression. He'd lowered the gun and pushed past us all.

He went over to a metal container on the floor and flipped it open. Inside were several of what appeared to be drinking straws.

He put the gun down and began looking at them one by one, holding each of them up to the light.

Ernesto knelt beside him, doing the same thing.

"Ruined," Bell was saying, tossing straw after straw aside. "The semen is ruined." He sounded as though he were about to sob. "The semen is ruined and Sturmgeist is dead." He had that strangled about-to-cry voice. I decided not to tell him about Wolf's fax.

I also thought that Jeet and I could start backing out, because the door to the freezer was wide open, and Hans and Ernesto were so preoccupied with the straws, but no.

The burro man, who until now had been keeping a very low profile, chose to act. In one dazzlingly swift motion, he plunged forward and grabbed the great big gun that Hans Bell had laid aside.

Hans and Ernesto, crying over spilt seed, still did not realize this.

"Out of the frying pan . . ." I muttered to Jeet.

The burro man heard me and smiled. "I like you, Heather Locklear," he said, still clipped and veddy British. "You've got spunk."

CHAPTER 14

One week later we are back at Primrose Farm on our patio. Jeet is basting something with his secret homemade barbecue sauce and he's saying, "So I'm thinking, here's this *new* guy with a gun, and *he's* so crazy that he's calling Robin Heather Locklear, and . . ."

And our guests, Lola and Cody, are squealing as though that's the funniest, farthest-fetched thing they've ever heard, which doesn't exactly thrill me.

But I let Jeet finish the story anyway, the arrival of Ramon Pedras. *He* had been the person the burro man had called. In fact, Pedras and Interpol had been onto the theft and were trying to pin down specifics when I'd come on the scene. So anyway, I listened as Jeet described the arrival of Pedras and his merry men and the unceremonious carting away of Ernesto Quinto and Hans Bell.

Jeet gives Lola and Cody the short version, but let me spin it out in detail for you:

I immediately click onto the Heather Locklear reference, just as Bell grabs Ernesto and uses him as a shield. "Oh, please, no," Ernesto is saying, so softly that I fear Jeet's prediction of a heart attack might be true.

But I am standing beside Bell, practically, and just then I feel the weight of the gun that I took from the burro man in the pocket of my dress.

I reach in and I hold the gun against Hans Bell's temple. I mean, my hand isn't even trembling. And I say, "Give it up."

I don't think Jeet likes remembering this part. And it kind of scares me, too. Because I was very, very serious.

Nothing happened to test my resolve, because it was at that precise moment that Officer Pedras came on the scene.

The burro man said it was about time.

And I said, tough to the very end, "Read them their rights."

It was Pedras's response that broke me free of whatever it was that had taken hold of me. "Rights?" he asked. And then just like at the end of some murder tra-la on television, we all had a good laugh.

All except the perps.

Whatever Jeet is making smells exceedingly good. I peer at the grill and see a mosaic of shrimp and scallops and fresh vegetables.

"But," I finish, "the stallion, Sturgmeist, is alive and well, it turns out. Because Wolf faxed a warning to the new owner in Argentina before he"— meaning Wolf—"got shot."

He and Marilee. But I don't say that. I don't want to conjure up the memory of poor Marilee lying there dead, or poor Wolf twitching. But the thing that Officer Pedras said really scared me, which was, that the son of the Nazi guy in Argentina would have dealt with both of them—Wolf and Marilee—in a really really bad way. So it was a blessing, sort of, in a way.

"Tell them about the *turista* medicine, Robin," Jeet prompts me.

"Oh, yeah," I said, glad to look again on the brighter side of the thing. So I told them about how Ernesto was so purple with outrage at his arrest and especially about being stuffed into the backseat of a Volkswagen.

I'd consoled him by digging the small bottle I had stashed in my dress pocket out and telling him, "Here, knock yourself out."

He took it greedily and started to glug it down, having first made some comment about what a fine liqueur it was.

Except that one of the policemen who had come to the scene snatched it away from him and, with one sniff, recognized the stuff for what it was.

"All of the police began making fun of Ernesto, the mighty gourmet, unmercifully," I said now.

"Which," Jeet added to the story, laughing so hard there were tears in his eyes, "I think was harder on Ernesto than the arrest itself."

"He was absolutely mortified," I said.

"But what about those young horses?" Lola asked. "What happens to them?"

"They're still trying to sort that out. Argentina and Mexico. That guy down in LaGrange, Kent something, is trying to buy some of them, too."

"Could revitalize the Mexican economy," Cody offered.

"It's a real mess," Jeet said. "And the thing is, I can still remember Robin standing there in our hotel room saying, 'It isn't as though I'm going to get involved in an international incident or anything.' "

"That," said Lola, "is when you should have known."

Everyone looked at me, expecting a snappy response, but I was frozen there, thinking.

Yes!

I dashed inside to the phone, Lola running behind me asking, "What? What is it?"

I ignored her and called Len Reasoner at the vet clinic. It was he who had told me about the man in LaGrange making some bid for the Sturmgeist stock.

"Len," I said. "Who adopted Marilee's Chihuahuas? And don't say a word about my upbringing or my mother."

"Tarnation," he said. "That was years ago."

"You have a computer. Just put the name of that breeder in LaGrange up on the screen."

"Hold your horses," he said.

I heard some clicking and then he told me, Kent Heimlich, LaGrange, Texas.

Heimlich! "He's related to Wolf," I said. "I knew they needed an American contact. Probably to sell the horses here. And that Kent something has some fancy mare, too." Of course, that explained how Marilee and Wolf had met in the first place, which had perplexed me. "Wolf was probably Kent's brother!"

"Huh?" the vet said.

Embryo transplants! I thought, and said, "I'll tell you later. And thanks."

"What should we do?" Lola asked me.

"I'm not sure. We'll have to figure this out." I mean, maybe this Kent person was in San Miguel, one of the disappearing tourists I'd seen at the overlook when I'd first talked to Felipe. Maybe Kent owned Milagro. Pedras was probably on top of that, though.

"But what made you even think that this Kent person could be involved?" Lola asked.

"I don't know. I thought about Marilee. And of course that made me think about her dogs. And then I realized that the dogs in Mexico were the *exact same dogs* she'd had up here. Now, come on, Lola, think about it. Do you really believe that someone other than Marilee would have wanted those dogs?"

"Everything okay in there?" Jeet called.

"Just fine," I shouted back. I gave Lola a shush sign, for now.

"Are you going to tell Jeet?" she whispered.

"Are you nuts?" I asked. "I mean, he's laughing now, but if I were to keep digging into this . . ."

"Plus you'd have to talk to the hunk again."

"What hunk?"

"Jimmy Smits," she said.

"God," I said, my face flushing. "Jimmy Smits—I mean Ramon Pedras—is the last person on my mind."

Jeet was in the doorway now. "You'd better believe it," he said. He had his big teak salad forks, one in each hand. "I can't see Robin lusting after a man who wields a screwdriver, when she knows what I can do with these."

He stood away from the door and tossed the forks in the air. Like magic forks, forks that had been beguiled, they somersaulted all around each other before they came back down and he caught them again.

The sunlight was slanted behind him, so that he was kind of framed in a golden glow.

Cody came up behind him and Lola and I stepped closer. The glow had enveloped all of us, I realized.

"I'll tell Len Reasoner everything I know," I said. "He can take it from here."

Carolyn Banks

Published by Fawcett Books.
Available in your local bookstore.